RETURN OF THE LIVING PROOF
Neighborlee Book 9

Michelle L. Levigne

www.YeOldeDragonBooks.com

Ye Olde Dragon Books
P.O. Box 30802
Middleburg Hts., OH 44130

www.YeOldeDragonBooks.com

2OldeDragons@gmail.com

Welcome to Neighborlee, Ohio.

Where? Somewhere on the North Coast of Ohio, south of Cleveland, right off I-71, north of Medina, in the heart of Cuyahoga County.

What is it? That's a little harder to explain.

Neighborlee is a place you need to experience.

The most important thing you need to understand: Neighborlee is *magic*. Some people say the town is alive. It exists to protect the weird and wonderful (and sometimes a little bit scary) from the cold, practical, material world.

More important, Neighborlee protects the outside world from the weird and wonderful that come to visit ... and sometimes come to stay.

First stop: Divine's Emporium, a four-story Victorian house sitting on a hill overlooking the Metroparks. Whatever you really need, you can find at Divine's. Even if you don't know what you're looking for when you walk in the door. The shop is often bigger inside than it is outside. Angela is the proprietor. Please stay on the first floor. You don't want to find out what is hidden and locked safely away upstairs. Like Aslan, Angela is good, but that doesn't mean she's safe. And neither are the secrets and wonders and doorways to other worlds that she protects ... and keeps securely locked.

Come in and explore. Meet the people who help Angela guard Neighborlee. Share their adventures of magic and wonder, danger and sacrifice. You never know who or what you'll run into as you walk the streets and listen to the stories of their lives.

NOTE:

In previous stories, you've met John Stanzer, the local PI, seeking other refugees from his home dimension, known as the Hunt.

*The stories about **The Hunt**, starting with **Dawn Memories**, are a YA fantasy series published by Writers Exchange. In **Return of the Living Proof**, you get some glimpses of Stanzer's struggle to find and catch up with Dawn, and start to put together a few more clues to what happened to the other members of the Hunt.*

Chapter One

Sometimes, I seriously consider never going beyond the border of Neighborlee. Not even for vital supplies that our local stores don't carry, like gourmet dark chocolate or loose leaf tea. With the strengthening of the protective field of magic around our town, the tendency was increasing for creeps and enemies to try to take stabs at us when we stepped outside, because it was getting harder for them to get in. Or the creeps and hopeful allies of Big Ugly (in theory, at least) parked on the borders of our town and settled in to plot against us. Such as the house on the border of Darbyville and Neighborlee, that tried to take a bite out of Angela my freshman year of college. (Still haven't quite recovered from that yet. Me, not her.)

That spring after Maurice came to town, the attacks started slowly. Actually, the attacks resumed, but we didn't know it at the time. There was a lot going on that summer, with hopeful part-time jobs and renewed weirdness in the college dorms, pregnant pseudo-dogs and our very own Neighborlee brand of time travel.

It started with a really lame attempt to steal my Jeep. This reinforced my belief that shopping should be conducted via computers, rather than in person.

I was coming back from a meeting of the advisory council for Sheridan Communications, driving from Independence, and remembered I needed some groceries. There was a new discount grocery store I wanted to check out that lay on the route between the office and home, so I thought I'd be semi-efficient and stop there. I was tired, and I should have listened to myself when I considered leaving the shopping for another day. Maybe I was too tired to be thinking clearly, or paying attention to that niggling sense of warning that should have been screaming in my ear. Honestly, I just wasn't paying the kind of attention I should have been employing 'round the clock, thanks to all the weirdness the guardians had encountered over the last couple years. That lack of alertness probably also gave off some vibes that marked me as an easy target. Maybe I was depending too much on that tendency for people's eyes to kind of skitter away from physically handicapped people they encounter in public. In essence, my own kind of cloaking field, without needing to steal it from the Romulans or employ evil magic.

I parked and dropped my keys when I slid out of the driver's seat. Another warning sign, maybe? I left them there on the console between the seats instead of putting them in my pocket immediately. In my own defense, I did hesitate, but I didn't get any shivers of warning, so I kept going. I hauled my chair out of the back seat, slung my backpack over the handle on the back of my chair, and reached back to the console to get my keys.

An arm in a long, black sleeve shoved me back so I fell into my chair, reached into my Jeep, and snatched at my keys.

Did I mention that besides being tired, I was getting a headache, and just waiting for an excuse to have a gripe fest?

I didn't care that I wasn't in Neighborlee, where people ignored weird things happening. I didn't care about that stupid unspoken rule not to attract attention with my broken semi-pseudo-superhero powers. I caught hold of my chair, turned around in time to see this idiot dressed all in black on a hot spring afternoon, and shoved him hard with my telekinesis. Nobody was carjacking **me**, dagnabbit!

He went down hard on the blacktop. Didn't make a sound. He just looked at me with his cold, pale blue eyes in a pale face, under all that wispy fine pale hair, and didn't even look angry. Well, that got me angry. I threw myself out of my chair, with a little mental push for extra impact, landed on him and pinned him, using a couple of moves I picked up from going to all my brother Pete's wrestling tournaments. He should have screamed, because I got him with my knee right in his gut. Nothing but a grunt.

I snatched at my keychain clutched in his fist. For a second, there was this spark when bare skin touched bare skin, and then it stung like that time I got accidentally doused with liquid fertilizer. That just made me angrier. I didn't feel sorry about my knee in his gut. He snarled something that didn't sound like English. Finally, a warning shiver down my back that sent a few roots of ice into my gut. About time my instincts woke up.

Then the laughing started. And hoots. And running feet. I wasn't invisible. Another reason to stay within the borders of

Neighborlee, maybe? Definitely, this was not my day.

None of the guys who helped me back into my chair were cute. Also, none of them believed in durable deodorant on a hot spring day. Why do guys wear tank tops and get greasy-sweaty and smell like sour metal at six in the afternoon? On the positive side, they sat on the creep who tried to steal my Jeep, came close to breaking his hand to get my keychain back, and mocked him mercilessly for letting a little crippled woman get the best of him. Most important, they kept him prisoner until a cop showed up.

A cop who called me "Ma'am." Seriously? Did I look old enough to get a "Ma'am" from a cop? I repeat: *Not my day*. About then I was getting nostalgic for my friends on the Neighborlee police force. Of course, if we were in Neighborlee, this lame carjacking never would have happened. Nobody in my town would have had the guts to even try. Here, though, I was just a little crippled woman.

The cop wasted time trying to talk me into going to the emergency medical clinic right there in the strip mall. While his back was turned, trying to convince me that I was in shock and didn't know that I was hurt from tussling with the carjacker, the too-pale creep in his black clothes vanished from the back seat of the patrol car.

Weird, huh? Creepy. Especially since stuff like that shouldn't happen outside of the borders of Neighborlee.

At least he didn't get my keychain. Pete made it for me that first summer after Mum and Pop adopted him. He used some incredible terra cotta beads his mother, Emma, had found when we were ransacking a secondhand store the last time we met up with the Crowders. They had bits of silver and chips of green and blue glass embedded in them. I loved that keychain. It just felt good in my hand, as well as a nice memory of Emma. Mum had a bracelet and earrings of the same beads that Emma had made for her before she and Jake were killed. I think if the creep had succeeded, I would have been more upset about the keychain than my Jeep getting stolen. I could replace the Jeep, but not those beads and the memories.

A couple of the people who came running when I tackled the guy were wannabe paparazzi, and they pulled out their phones. They got pictures of the creep and even some videos of me tackling him. The cop got them, and I asked for copies, to share with my favorite pet cop, Gordon. Hey, I was no dummy. When something weird happened, that was my cue to at least ask questions and be on the alert.

Especially since Gordon notified me later that evening that while my Jeep and my features were clear in the video, the creep was just a blur. We had to wonder if there was a branch of the Rivals that had survived the implosion and self-destruction that caught up with them last summer, and the survivors were gunning for me. They at least knew better than to try to exact revenge on me, or any of the guardians, inside Neighborlee.

Another reason not to leave the safe borders of town.

So was it any wonder that the next day, I woke up with that sensation of I-had-a-dream-but-can't-remember-it-to-warn-me-something-is-going-to-happen? Felicity didn't have any weird dreams. Ford, Athena and Doni Longfellow didn't have weird dreams. Kurt and Jane didn't have weird dreams. So whatever was going on, maybe it was just focused on me?

It wasn't one of those something-is-chewing-on-the-roots-of-the-town dreams, so maybe Big Ugly wasn't waking up? Hopefully, he still had indigestion from swallowing up all those agents of the Rivals and that gas they were pumping into Eden, last summer.

So what was the dream about?

I was looking for weird stuff, but I ignored the armies of plastic gnomes, flamingoes, and clowns appearing in people's front lawns throughout town. For one thing, that had been happening for more than a month. We had gotten flyers in the newspaper and in the mail, encouraging us to use the services of a new company called Pi Surprise to celebrate special occasions. The lawn decorations were a resurgence of a fad that had been big when I was in high school. Essentially, Pi Surprise filled people's lawns in the early morning hours with all sorts of trendy decorations and a lighted sign, to drawn attention to whatever big event was happening in the house. Birthday. Anniversary. Graduation. Joining the military. Birth of a baby. Wedding.

I didn't consider the lawn clutter in the same category of "weird" that the guardians needed to deal with. They were more irritating than weird. What's the dividing line between kitschy and tacky? However, after that dream, the rows of flamingos, clowns, penguins, and gnomes took on a sinister look, for me. I had heard for years there were people who thought clowns were creepy. Now I finally understood. Those gnomes were worse, though. They weren't the typical garden decoration gnomes. These were kind of wrinkly and bug-eyed and those eyes seemed to be following me when I drove past, or when I wheeled past. How come those gnomes showed up more than all the other characters used in those cheesy, lame congratulation announcements all put together?

Soon, though, I had more important things to worry about. I had my first blue storm dream. At first, I didn't remember the dreams when I woke up. So how did I know I was having them? Right. Well, I was waking up with the feeling that I had dreamed, and that dream was important, but it didn't make me itch on the underside of my skin like that dream I had right after the failed Jeep-jacking. Experience had taught me if it was important, I would remember something out of that dream, even if it was so misty that I only had a sense of déjà vu. So how come I wasn't remembering details of dreams, while at the same time knowing I had dreamed, and the contents were important?

Felicity and Jane and I discussed it over lunch and agreed that if I kept having dreams but not remembering, I needed to get help. Either a physical, to deal with a chemical imbalance of some kind. Or … ask Angela to request a house call from her purple-garbed Fae doctor friend, who had helped me before. Because something was blocking my memories.

The third morning I woke up with the same sensation of having dreamed, with a strong dose of confusion added to the mix. It was a sunny day and the grass and driveway were dry. I fully expected to look outside and see everything drenched, with branches on the lawn from the fierceness of the storms. At least now I knew I was dreaming about bad weather.

So I checked with the rest of the guardians, sending emails before work and making phone calls during the day. They all responded within an hour or two. Kurt wasn't having storm dreams. Jane wasn't having storm dreams. Ford wasn't having storm dreams. I wasn't even going to ask Felicity. I was pretty sure all her long-lasting newlywed bliss would have driven away every bad dream even if Big Ugly was about to physically manifest and erupt into our dimension through her cellar.

I could have called Angela and asked her. However, when it came to weird dreams and anything that might be a harbinger of trouble, it was always better to talk to her face-to-face. The sooner, the better. Experience had taught us that no matter how flimsy the niggling sense of something being "off," no matter how few details we had, it was just plain foolish not to start asking questions and comparing notes immediately. This was Neighborlee, the weirdness capital of the state, country, planet, and possibly the universe. When it came to the continuing efforts of interdimensional nasties to invade Earth, and our never-ending battle as guardians to make sure that never happened, the only stupid question was the one we didn't ask.

"Storms are always symbolic," Angela said, when I finally got to Divine's after work. We settled on the swing in her backyard. The late afternoon light and shadows crept across the long meadow of the Metroparks at the bottom of the hill where Divine's Emporium sat.

Maurice was keeping guard over the shop, in case anyone stopped in during the last hour or two before closing. Not that he could actually make a sale or answer any questions, since about ninety-nine percent of the residents of Neighborlee couldn't see or hear him. He could still pop out to the backyard and let Angela know if anyone needed her help. Life was kind of tough for the guy, just being shrunk down to five inches tall, with wings slapped on his back Tinkerbell wouldn't be caught dead in. Add in being invisible and inaudible to anyone without a hefty dose of something magical or supernatural? I liked the guy, just for holding up so well in a pretty rough situation.

"If I was getting a warning, shouldn't I remember some details?" I asked. That question had been coalescing in my brain for the last few hours. I was getting a little worried that Big Ugly had figured out that we were able to eavesdrop on his planning sessions, and he had found a way to at least turn down the volume, if not block us entirely.

"Yes, you should. So maybe it's not a warning, or at least not eavesdropping on our enemy's latest plotting." She sighed and pursed her lips, and her gaze went distant. "Maybe the storms are a physical manifestation of some disturbance in ..." A shrug, and one corner of her mouth quirked up. "I can't believe I'm saying this.

You and your Star Trek friends are a bad influence on me." Another sigh, a sparkle in her eyes. "Essentially a disturbance in the Force."

"Please don't mix universes on us," I said with a groan, but I grinned. If Angela could tease, even if a little bit, then whatever was bothering me wasn't that serious. At least, I hoped not.

"Nothing worse than a purist." She shook her head. Then went very still, that "listening" expression making her gaze turn distant for a moment. "Perhaps that is what it is. Universes … mixing. Yes, storms are a physical manifestation of universes, or perhaps more accurately, dimensions coming into contact, or conflict, or at the very least intersecting."

I bit my lip to keep from blurting a stupid question, such as asking if the whole premise of the Nine Realms coming into alignment, from the second Thor movie, was happening to us. Please, not nine different dimensions of reality. Two would be bad enough, hard enough to deal with.

"Athena is spending the day here tomorrow. She and Wallace are going to spend the premier week for Bethany's new movie with her, and she's going to ransack the vintage clothing room to put together outfits. I will ask her to contact London. Monitoring the weather, both on Earth and out in space, is something better suited to her skills."

"So what do we do if it really is an invasion from space? Like, if the invaders are coming from that direction, dropping on us instead of bursting up from beneath us?"

"We can't be sure that unplanned or unannounced visitors from other dimensions are always bad. All we can do is be watchful, pay attention to the warnings we do get … and hope that we don't go to the extremes of either response."

"Meaning?"

A twitch of her lips seemed to trigger something in my head, and I remembered. In my defense at being so slow on the uptake, it had been a really hectic day at the paper. Conrad and Clarice were out of town on vacation, a second honeymoon of all things, and as copy editor I was nominally in charge. So of course, all the wackos and conspiracy theory nutcases and gripers and complainers descended on the newspaper office within ten minutes of them leaving the state of Ohio. How come people who didn't live in Neighborlee, who didn't even live in Cuyahoga County, decided the *Neighborlee Tattler* had to cover their miniscule problems with the local government, the trash pickup, their disputes with their neighbors, or new proof that the guy living next door was head of a sleeper cell for a new generation of Nazis?

Angela's words "extremes of either response" triggered memories of a long, fun, silly discussion we had at our last Trek party. She had come for our Rites of Spring picnic and provided a trunk full of science fiction and fantasy memorabilia, collectibles, and hard-to-find books as prizes for our games. Near the end of the fun and silliness, as we gathered around several fire pits against the evening chill, we had grown somewhat philosophical in our exhaustion. Amazing, the odd directions our minds could go when we were tired and yet still hyped on too much sugar and junk food and the fun of letting go and being kids for a handful of hours.

I was sitting around one firepit with Gordon, Mandy, Daniel, and Angela. Maurice wasn't with us, but hanging with Doni, Athena, and Meggie. Between the three girls, he was able to participate in the discussion. And from the laughter and sometimes shrieks, it was a great one. Maurice couldn't be heard by Meggie, but he could be felt, so he sat on her shoulder and tapped out Morse code to her, while the other two girls could hear him.

My firepit group's discussion centered on the movies dealing with aliens descending on planet Earth. To enslave, to help, to investigate, to destroy, to make us pets, to eat us, to find something hidden on Earth, on and on. We agreed that there seemed to be a tendency among Humans, or at least the people writing the movie scripts, to go to extremes in responding to the appearance of aliens among us. Which might explain why so many movies about alien visitations showed them sneaking around, trying to keep their presence a secret, or else dropping from the sky with outright deceptions or huge machines to wipe out all life on Earth. We either made the mistake of welcoming the aliens with open arms, and getting our world ripped out from underneath us. Or we made the mistake of considering alien visitors a threat that had to be annihilated while the ship was still at the edge of the solar system, if at all possible.

"So," I said now in Angela's backyard, with that discussion in mind, "you're saying we should wait for proof that they're out to suck our brains or help us transcend to the next level of existence before we either put out the welcome mat or fire a fifty-megaton pulsar cannon?"

"That approach has always worked for me," Angela said after a brief pause to think.

"So do we wait to tell Col. Hayward, or wait until he contacts us and asks what we've been picking up?"

"Wait until we have something concrete. Something besides a few dreams that don't leave any residue to examine."

So that was what we did.

I had a lot on my mind when I got home from work that evening, but not enough to keep me from seeing the gnomes and some really warped, glittery, pink winged creatures that might have been Andy Warhol's version of the Sugarplum Fairy. They were scattered among a half-dozen lawns across the street from my house. No signs, no announcements of celebrations or congratulations. I slowed down as I drove past, and got a really good chill up my back, when it looked like one of the gnomes turned on its stake and seemed to be watching me.

Todd, who owned the house three doors down with more gnomes than faeries, pulled up behind me and turned into his driveway as I headed for my driveway. I was just enough of a reporter, and just irritated enough with those weird critters, I had to satisfy my curiosity. He was still standing in his driveway, hands on his hips, when I had parked, got my chair out, and wheeled down to the end of the driveway to call over to him.

"What's up with you folks?" I asked, when I had caught his attention.

"Heck if I know. We didn't order this stuff. Think maybe someone else had this, and some kids are pulling pranks, warming up for Senior Prank Night?"

That would explain it, and part of me hoped that was it. I asked him to let me know what he found out, and went inside the house. Pete came home from a studying session with Meggie and Doni, and reported that Todd and the people from the houses on either side of him were busy pulling up the gnomes and faeries and tossing them in one of the wheeled garbage bins.

Someone came from Pi Surprise long after dark, in a windowless van, to collect their property. According to Todd, they claimed yes, some kids must have been pranking, because the figures were taken from several houses on the border of Darbyville. Whoever it was took the time to walk around to all the houses on our street and put flyers for Pi Surprise in our mailboxes. Not just advertising their services, but announcing they were hiring. It was good timing, in terms of getting the attention of kids before they made any commitments for summer jobs. But bad timing, considering the hassle of all those lawn ornaments populating lawns where they didn't belong.

Pete rescued the job openings flyer from the recycling bin. I stopped myself just in time from asking him not to apply. First of all, because even though both my brothers were good guys, chances were good Pete would apply if I asked him not to. And second, he really did need another source of income, because his relationship with Meggie Richards was getting pretty serious. Which meant he needed money for dates.

Looking back, I should have told him not to apply, and been ready to argue with him. As it was, Pete didn't act on it right away. He found another job that he started before school let out for the summer, and I soon had other things on my mind.

Just about the time the little ruckus with Jon-Tom Castle, Jeri Hollis and the baby left on her doorstep had cleared up, late in June, I started remembering bits and pieces, enough to term them blue dreams. London had also picked up some details from the weather tracking satellites. Don't ask me how she penetrated all the layers of security around those satellites without setting off alarms.

I dreamed about blue storms. Long streaks of light that weren't lightning. Churning in the sky. A matching churning in my gut.

London gathered up data on what the scientists were calling a storm in space. The problem was, they couldn't pinpoint a location or at least an origin point for the energy ripples and reverberations. One of them likened it to being in a series of canyons, and hearing echoes. The echoes bounced around so much there was no way to determine the origin of the sound that started all the echoes. For all anyone could guess, the storm that created the reverberations and fascinating readings, which they might be studying for years, had likely ended years earlier.

With that information, it was time to call a guardians meeting at Divine's. We only had to talk for maybe ten minutes before we agreed to send the information London had gathered to Hayward.

If we were going to get an interdimensional visitation, and all that energy meant something was trying to break through from another layer of reality, then he needed to be warned. Yeah, we were really kind, dumping the weight of deciding who to tell and how and when on his shoulders. (Sarcasm, here.) Well, he was our only link with the military and the higher-ups in the government who would have to deal with an alien invasion. If they were able to deal with the invasion on a physical level, of course.

We also agreed to send the information to Hoax. Jane took care of that, and Daniel made sure his grandfather and his council had copies of the data, so they could start pulling in information from their sources and compare what readings and warnings and reactions their people were getting.

Then I gave my teeny tiny report on the change in my dreams.

Stanzer dropped his coffee cup when I said, "blue."

"You're sure? Blue storms?" His voice was strained, and I doubted it was from the scorching of coffee soaking into his pants.

"That's the impression I got. I'm not really seeing anything ..." I forgot what I was about to say, mesmerized by the blue sparks that trickled along the lines of the scars on his right wrist.

Those scars were made by the teeth of the Hounds, when the interdimensional guardian angel-type beasties dragged Stanzer and other children from their world to Earth.

Before I could take a breath and ask if anyone else saw the blue sparks, they were gone. I met Stanzer's gaze. Licked my lips.

"Yeah, just an impression of storms and ..." I shrugged. "Blue."

"So no good to ask you where you thought the storms were." He looked down at the spreading stain on his pants. They were khaki, lightweight for summer, not coffee or chocolate brown, so he wasn't going to get away with a big coffee stain.

"But we should take it as a sign of hope." Angela rested her hand on his, which was gripping his empty cup tight enough to make it creak.

With a little urging from Angela, Stanzer told us what he could remember of the storm and the journey from his home dimension, pulled through time and space by the Hounds. I had seen a Hound, and once was more than enough for me. It was something like a wolf, tall enough that its head and shoulders were even with Stanzer's. It had helped save my life two Christmases ago. Jay

Parker had tried to run me over when I was crossing the street. The Hound had picked me up and carried me to safety in just two seconds flat.

Felicity took notes, and we passed the information on to London and Sherwood, to help them narrow down the search that they had been conducting for more than a year now, trying to find more members of the Hunt. That was the name of the children who had been given into the protection of the Hounds. Stanzer was sure, in that kind of certainty that had a strong element of desperation, the blue storms were a sign of members of the Hunt gathering together, or Hounds at work, protecting members of the Hunt.

"Or Gahlmorag could be coming through," he admitted, somewhat reluctantly.

"That doesn't sound good," Jake offered.

"Sounds like a good name for a galactic despot in RPG," Gordon offered. That earned a sigh and rolled eyes, followed by a grin, from Mandy.

The two of them were into RPG, otherwise known as role-playing games. Some smart-aleck in our Trek club had given them a deluxe RPG set for a wedding present, of all things, and they had become addicted.

"Actually, that about sums up Gahlmorag," Stanzer said. "He surrounded our world and basically demanded all the children of the ruling houses be handed over to him as hostages. We have Talents, born into different bloodlines. Our ruling families use what Hamin gives us to help our people. Healers, visionaries, other gifts. It's a stewardship, a duty, not a privilege. At least, that's how most of the clan heads see it."

Chapter Two

Stanzer shook his head and gave us a crooked little smile. It struck me that this was something he had been thinking about for a long time. Probably going over everything he had been taught before all the children were sent away, just to make sure he remembered. He probably needed to talk to someone about it, yet it might feel odd to him at the same time. Just like it would feel odd to us, if we discussed what it meant to be guardians with people who weren't guardians, and especially people who didn't live in Neighborlee.

"Our parents chose to give us into Hamin's service and entrust our safety to the Hounds," he continued after a brief, thoughtful pause, "and sent us away. All these years, I haven't found another member of the Hunt. It's part of why I became an investigator, to develop the connections to help me search." He shrugged and gave us a weary, brave smile. "Now, though, with those storms …"

"Think we should get the Colonel involved, too?" Kurt asked. "If we've got aliens preparing to land on Earth, he ought to know. Especially if there's some Sith Lord, or worse, sniffing out your trail."

Angela agreed with us and sent the same information to Col. Hayward.

Just two days later, Hayward responded with information, classified for now because of its oddness: images of churning, unusual weather patterns in the area of the Bermuda Triangle. What looked like the "seeds" of hurricanes, there one moment, with streaks of electric blue going through them, and then gone just a few heartbeats later. And no signs that anything had been disturbed, other than broken palm fronds or foam on the water.

I might have found some hope, to share with my brothers. The disturbances that seemed to be tied into Lost Kids or Hunt activity were in the vicinity of the Triangle. However, there was a big blank area, clearly visible once the locations of all the disturbances were marked onto one map. Smack dab in the middle of that blank area was the hotel where my parents had been staying when they vanished. And, as Daniel had revealed to us last summer, where his grandfather, Arthur, had been staying. He had been in Bermuda at the same time as my parents, following up his own research. We were all disappointed to learn that he hadn't been there to meet my folks or pursue a similar line of research. It was all luck. Maybe bad luck on Arthur's part. He had been knocked flat by something that was still inexplicable, about the same time my folks vanished. He had been drained physically, and his memory of several days wiped away. Arthur had taken months to recover.

Of course, Neighborlee sat in the middle of a big blank area, too. All sorts of electrical energy and disturbances, and our town was in the proverbial eye of the storm.

Kind of makes you wonder, you know?

~~~~~

Just a few days after that, Maurice rode over to my house on Cerb. I hadn't seen my guardian hound-angel for a while, and one look at the smaller, cuter hound sitting next to him told me why.

"Cerb, you dog." I couldn't help it.

The hound was a girl, and since she was visibly pregnant, chances were good she was the sweetheart for whom Cerb had taken voluntary exile and guardian service on Earth.

He snorted and his mouth fell open, tongue lolling out extra long, with lots of drool. His gross way of laughing at me. Maybe getting back at me for the teasing.

"Hey, Lanie," Maurice said, and leaped off Cerb's back to hover in front of me. I knew he was uncomfortable with all the sparkle and glitter of his wings, which were part of his punishment when he was exiled to Earth, but watching them go at nearly sonic speed to keep him hovering was … mesmerizing. "We need your help."

"Felicity is as close as you're going to get to an OB-GYN for … well, anthropomorphic interdimensional travelers."

"No, not that." He swallowed and looked a little green for a few seconds. The color hovered longest in the tips of his tiny pointed ears. The guy was only five inches tall, but that was a vibrant shade that just stayed visible. "At least, not yet. Loralee isn't due to pop for another month."

Cerb made a sound somewhere between a cough, a choke, and a grunt.

"At least, we hope. We need a safe place for her to hole up until
~~~~~

the demon spawn are born."

So help me, I wished I had a fly swatter. I knew Maurice liked Cerb, so he wouldn't say something like that unless he was either in a viciously snarky mood, or he was joking. Still, I wanted to hit him hard enough to send him all the way to home plate at Progressive Field. Considering how far away we were from Downtown, that would take a lot of muscle power, aided by my telekinetic talent. I was sure I could manage it. How dare he say something like that about babies who hadn't been born yet?

Unless he wasn't joking?

"Umm, Maurice … what will the babies look like when they're born? Do they take after the physical bodies of their parents, or are they …" I couldn't finish the question. I looked into Loralee's big amethyst eyes and I couldn't find the words.

Yeah, ever heard of a normal, ordinary dog with amethyst eyes? Proof she was otherworldly.

What I wanted to know, but didn't dare ask at that time, was why some extra-dimensional visitors had to take on terrestrial forms, and their limitations, such as Cerb and Loralee, while others, like Maurice, went around in their own bodies? Although, granted, in the case of Maurice, with some modifications.

Instead, I thought for a few seconds, then said, "Harry moved into Felicity's place. Would his old room be good enough? Not much furniture to move around. Put the mattress on the floor, or would they want to sleep on the bed at normal height?"

Maybe I gave in too fast. On the other hand, this was a pregnant woman, even if she didn't look like one. I owed Cerb for protecting my neck a few times last year.

"Are there any special arrangements they need?" I hated talking to Maurice when Cerb and Loralee were right there. I had gone through situations just like this after I landed in my wheelchair. Too many people had a tendency to want to talk over or around someone in a wheelchair or showing other handicaps. They seemed to prefer to deal with the able-bodied person with the gimp, instead of talking directly to the gimp. Kind of rude. I didn't want to do that to them. Since they couldn't talk to me, I had to ask Maurice, who was clearly there as go-between.

"Just a place to get out of the darkness. There's a kind of a clash of magics and resonances, so it's a little uncomfortable to stay at

Divine's for too long once the sun goes down. Don't ask. I don't understand."

Cerb snorted and Loralee gave a little whine.

"Yeah, neither do they. Probably some side effect of staying so long in these bodies. Anyway, during the day, they'll be on patrol, although Loralee will probably spend a lot of the next couple weeks getting off her feet, down in the park, or at Divine's." Maurice shrugged. "They've never been through this, I sure as heck haven't been through this before, so … we're all guessing."

Pete came home while I was settling the expectant parents in Harry's old room. He was pretty excited to see Cerb, then tripped over his tongue and nearly tripped over his own feet a few times when he saw Loralee and realized what was going on. He didn't say it, but he gave Cerb the "you dog" look. It was kind of funny.

Once we had things set up to Loralee's liking, she and Cerb and Maurice headed out again. They were on patrol, after all, making sure that inimical forces on Earth didn't hear the lying siren song of Big Ugly like the Rivals had, and come into our town to try to help him break through to invade Earth.

Pete's timing was good, because there was furniture to move around and put into storage. Not much, since Harry had moved almost everything he owned into Felicity's place, after she and Jake finished renovating their house and moved out. Sometimes I did miss that ridiculous espresso machine. The furniture in Harry's old room was simple, meant for guests. Pete moved the desk out, and we turned the dresser drawers upside down so they became stairs, so Loralee could climb up onto the bed. I had a few squeamish moments, imagining her giving birth and soaking the mattress. Well, it was a spare bed. I would worry about replacing a mattress when I needed to replace it, and not before.

Pete and I put some time in searching through my freezer and refrigerator, trying to figure out what to serve our guests for dinner. According to Maurice, Cerb and Loralee both liked ordinary Human food, and she had developed a taste for spicy cuisine in the last month. Great, a dog with a hankering for Szechuan or Mexican. It could have been worse. How would I explain a dog chowing down on pickles? Or chocolate? It was supposed to be poison in large quantities for dogs.

While we worked on dinner, Pete dropped his bomb: he had

lined up a second summer job. I bit my lip to keep from asking how he thought he was going to spend any time with Meggie, when he was working a second job. I had the feeling the second job was so he could take Meggie out on really nice dates. *sigh* My little brother was growing up and facing adult conundrums.

"What was that?" I had an awful urge to stick my pinkies in both ears and dig, because my brain didn't want to acknowledge what Pete had just told me.

"Pi Surprise." He sighed, like he had gone through this a few times already in his mind, and practicing hadn't helped.

"Why would you want to do that? Especially after Gordon told us about all the complaints they've been getting."

"Because it has to be done really early in the morning --"

"I repeat, why would *you* want to do it? You're the one who doesn't run on solar batteries, remember?"

Getting up early to bomb someone's lawn with decorations was part of the package. It had to be done early, so the workers wouldn't get caught and sent away by the unwilling recipients of the embarrassment.

"Because it won't get in the way of going out in the afternoon, and it'll never get in the way of my other job."

"Okay, that makes sense."

Pete turned to look at me, to make sure I wasn't being sarcastic.

"Are you able to handle the work on your bike? Because I'm not getting up at four-dark-thirty to drive you around. I'm proud of you that you're being responsible for your expenses … and I can't believe I'm sounding more and more like …" I laughed.

"You were going to say you sound like Mum and Pop, but you don't, because they would never talk like that," he said, sinking down into the nearest chair with a big grin.

"Just sounding like a parent. Man, is this what happens when there's a baby on the way? The air changes and does something to your brain so you start sounding like an adult?" I shook my head and held up a hand to stop him responding with whatever smart-aleck comeback was making him grin like that. "Okay, I'm proud of you. Even though you couldn't pay me enough to take a job like that. Staying up late to fly patrol is one thing, but getting up early? Nuh uh. Not me."

"I can take my bike or the moped to the office and then ride with the truck carrying the signs and stakes and all that stuff. No problem."

"How close are they?" I tried to remember seeing a sign for Pi Surprise. They hadn't come into the *Tattler* to buy advertising yet. Which suddenly struck me as a little strange. All their advertising was either in the *Plain Dealer*, or stuffed into mailboxes. Nothing in the local paper. So how far away was their office?

"They're in that little flower market on the corner down past the schools."

"On the Neighborlee side of the border, or the Allenby side?"

Pete thought a moment, while I held my breath and told myself it was all right, nothing dangerous ever came into Neighborlee from Allenby. Darbyville, yes, but not Allenby.

"Across the street, so I guess Allenby. I saw the help wanted sign just about the time they were putting it up in the window. It's a new office. They moved here from Euclid. So I'll spend the first couple weeks just helping with renovating the office."

"Okay. Sounds good." I told myself I was hungry, it had been a long day at work, and Pete would make a good spy, to figure out if there was something not-quite-ordinary going on with Pi Surprise. Maybe someone was just out to make things difficult for an expanding business, moving those gnomes around.

I knew the place Pete was talking about. The lot held a ramshackle building that had once been a convenience store and then went through at least a dozen transformations all the years I was growing up. It was in a bad location for businesses. The chunk of land set aside for Neighborlee schools sat right on the southern border of town. The building had started out as a gas station, just across the street and over the border in Allenby, nearly hidden by huge clumps of trees on three sides. Over the years, all those businesses that had moved in and moved out had neglected the building and the parking lot. It was generally a bad location for businesses that depended on visibility and traffic driving by to survive.

Thinking about it, I supposed a business that just used the building for a headquarters and sent its workers out would probably last longer than anything that had tried to set up there in the past. At the very least, Pete would have work for the summer. I couldn't imagine him keeping the job when school started again in the fall.

That night, Loralee woke up crying. I had the awful feeling she was sick, or maybe going into premature labor. Before I could get from my bed to my wheelchair, Cerb let out a howl that almost made me feel sorry for whoever had enraged him. Then he walked right through the wall from the guest room to my bedroom. He gave me a look that told me he was in defensive mode, then he leaped through my bedroom wall to go outside.

He stopped after that first howl, otherwise I might have had some irate neighbors to deal with. Harry got outside and was walking around the garage apartment and the rest of the yard by the time I got in my chair and to the door. He came up the ramp at the same time Cerb went back to the guestroom by going straight through the wall.

"Anything?" I asked, and backed up so Harry could come inside.

He stayed outside and shook his head. His forehead wrinkled up and his mouth twisted in a crooked grin, and I was pretty sure that shake wasn't a no, so much as it was admitting he wasn't quite sure what was going on.

"Could have sworn I saw something, but it scurried away before I could get close." He snorted. "Before Cerb could get to it. Something small. I'd say rabbits or groundhogs or something. We don't have skunks, do we?"

"Hope not."

"Yeah, well, there was a smell, but it wasn't skunk." He rubbed his nose. "It's gone now."

"Something worried Cerb."

"Yeah. I was really hoping ..." Harry shrugged and started backing down the ramp. He had left his door open and a flickering, bluish light spilled out, meaning he was watching a movie when Cerb raised the alarm.

"Hoping what?"

"That they really are camping here to give them a break from all the woo-woo magical fluctuations at Divine's."

"Why wouldn't they?"

He muttered something that I was pretty sure was Spanish his parents wouldn't have taught him.

"You could be the target again." He shrugged.

"Why wouldn't Cerb -- okay, why wouldn't Maurice tell me that's what Cerb was doing? What's different about now than last year?"

"Yeah, that's a consideration. Whatever was sneaking around, Cerb let them know they aren't getting in or doing anything." Harry scrubbed his face with his palms and let out a groan louder than Cerb had been. "Go back to sleep."

"Physician, heal thyself."

He stuck his tongue out at me and stepped into his apartment. A moment later the little light over the door turned off. I sat for a few moments longer, looking out over my yard, trying to hear or feel if anything was out of place. Then it occurred to me that the nightlight over the stove was bright enough to outline me in the doorway. Enough to make me a target.

Not a good feeling to have sitting on the threshold of my own house. I said a few silent prayers as I backed up and closed the door and made sure it was locked. When I turned to go down the hall, Cerb was sitting in the hallway, right by the little nightlight.

"Is it gone? Was it dangerous? Or just something being nosy?"

He thumped his tail against the wall a few times, then went to the guestroom door and nudged it open with his nose and went back in with Loralee. I muffled a chuckle. What sort of etiquette made him use the door when he was indoors, but when he was outdoors he didn't need to use a door?

I went back to bed and had a talk with God about all sorts of unanswered questions and the problem of not knowing the right questions, to help us figure out what was going on.

~~~~~

Two days later, Pete brought me the news that I had to sign his Pi Surprise employment contract, as his temporary guardian while our parents were still out of the country. We insisted on saying they were out of the country, rather than missing-with-no-clue-what-happened.

He was sixteen, going on seventeen. What kind of legal department did this company have, that they wouldn't let a guy his age sign his own employment contract? What kind of trouble had they run into in the past, that they needed legal adults to sign contracts for part-time work? For a few seconds after Pete gave me the news, I really hoped he would decide he didn't want to work
~~~~~

for these people.

"Okay, let me look it over."

"You have to come down to the office to sign it."

"Why?" I got a shiver of warning up my back that Pete's shrug for an answer just irritated.

"I asked. They said it was company policy. They said I could have a copy once it was signed, but not before."

Again, I waited for a few seconds, hoping he would tell me it was too much trouble, the people were weird, forget about it. No such luck, though.

The next day was a half-day, a paper delivery day, so I agreed to pick up Pete after lunch and go down to the Pi office with him to sign the contract. If I didn't find anything weird about it. On the way there, I suggested that he consider getting a part-time job as an assistant circulation manager, overseeing the delivery boys and girls, since he didn't mind getting up really early. He just gave me a withering look. Ah, for the good old days when he considered everything I said as pure wisdom. Well, maybe not everything. The kid paid attention better when he still had a clear memory of being thrown off that balcony over the river in England, and me leaping off after him and flying us both to safety.

The corner beyond the Neighborlee Schools property was in that nebulous area between farms and park land, a section of road that ended up being the long way around no matter what the destination was. That contributed to hardly anyone using it. Hence the business-killing dearth of traffic. The last business in there had been a flower market, and from the state of the building, it looked like it had been closed for ten years, not three.

"How long have they been renovating this place?" I had to ask, pausing just a few seconds longer than necessary at the flashing yellow light in front of the schools parking lot entrance. There was no traffic coming from any direction, so I didn't really need to do more than coast to a near-stop and then make my turn. I came to a full stop anyway, and studied the building sitting kitty-corner so it turned the parking lot into a triangle. That had to be awkward maneuvering. Maybe that contributed to the deaths of the previous businesses.

"Maybe two weeks?" Pete shrugged. Then he frowned and blinked and shook his head.

"What?" I didn't like the hint of a dazed look in his eyes.

"Didn't really notice before ..." Another shrug. "They're working on the inside, first."

Then how come the impression I got was that the windows inside were dirtier than outside? I couldn't see any lights through the grimy glass. There were cars parked on the far side of the building. When I pulled into the parking lot, I glimpsed a rental truck out back, and two people moving what looked like office furniture. I shuddered a little at the thought of them setting up an office in grimy surroundings. That reaction made no sense, because I'm not really that much of a neat-freak. This whole situation wasn't making a lot of sense. These people should have done more renovation work, at least fixed the sign on the corner, with broken panes in the lighted portion, and again, that sensation of grime clinging to everything. A long banner that might have been plastic sheeting covered the front face of the building, proclaiming it the new home of Pi Surprise Celebration Lawn Ornaments. In the window directly under the banner was a big sign declaring, "We're Hiring. Start Your Path to an Incredible Future Here."

Yeah, right. An incredible future getting up in the dark and cold maybe two mornings a week to stick dozens of flamingos or clowns or cows or storks or whatever in people's lawns.

Normally I wasn't that pessimistic, even if I was often that sarcastic. This place made me itch in a place I couldn't scratch because it was in my mind and spirit, not my body. That made me cranky. I was ready to tell Pete forget it, I wasn't going to let him work at a place like this.

Then two kids I knew from high school sports pulled into the parking lot. They were driving a beater car that had all the signs of being a high school kid's first car, bought with summer job money and held together with desperate prayers and chewing gum. On a second look, I recognized that car. It had been *mine* Pete's entire lifetime ago. Somehow, that cheered me up, that my first car would come into this parking lot like a sign that everything was okay. At least it didn't blow gaskets or make weird shrieking sounds of warning.

The boys jumped out of the car and looked around and recognized us. They waved. Pete waved back. Then he cringed.

"They're here to sign contracts too?" I asked. He nodded.

"They're two years older than you. They probably don't need an adult. Want me to stay out here until they're gone?"

He rolled his eyes and made that little grunting sound that usually stood in for a lot of things that he either couldn't or didn't dare put into words. This time I interpreted it as, "Thanks for not embarrassing me in front of the guys."

Pete got out and went into the building after the other two. I took my time getting out of my Jeep and pulling my wheelchair out of the back seat. They came out just as I dropped down into my seat and reached to push the door closed. They waved, I waved back, and waited as they pulled out of the driveway. A few memories made me smile. I had loved the feeling of independence I had with that beater car. I was glad it was still alive and serving another generation of high school kids learning to spread their wings. I just hoped my car would refuse to function when those boys chose to do something stupid.

I wheeled into the building. The door was propped halfway open. Once I got around it and could look inside, I had to admit Pete was right. The renovations were all interior for now. Fresh paint stung the air and brightened the inside. That wasn't dirt on the inside of the windows, but sheer curtains, kind of a grayish, peach-ish shade I wasn't sure I liked. Carpet squares covered the floor and seemed to grab at my wheels for a few seconds as I went to the far right of the door, where Pete stood in front of a desk.

The woman sitting there wore one of those power suits, all sharp angles and sleek lines, in a glossy, gray-black material. She was one of those pale blondes who would only need some blood-red lipstick and black eyeliner to be a convincing vampire in cosplay. Her name was Kerri, and her skin felt just a little too chill when we shook hands. Her smile was bright and warm, and so was her voice, and they just didn't seem to go with the rest of her. Yet she was polite, friendly, and apologized for the "silly legal necessities" that needed me to co-sign the contract with Pete.

The dang contract was ten sheets of paper, printed front and back. In pretty small font. I estimated it was maybe eight point, comparing it to the font we used at the newspaper. She offered us both pens, and I half-expected to find out the ink was red.

I never found out what color the ink was.

Cerb came tearing into the building, frisking and wriggling

and leaping up to put his front paws first on Pete's chest, then the arms of my chair. He pushed on my chair -- which was a pretty good trick, considering he pushed from the right side, but my chair started rolling backwards.

"Shoo! Get out! Where did that mangy thing come from?" Kerri's voice cracked as she stumbled out of her chair and reached for a phone book sitting on the shelving behind her desk. She heaved it at Cerb with pinpoint accuracy.

He dodged and the phone book bounced off my knee with a hard *thwack-crack.* I swore for a second that crack was my femur breaking. My whole leg went numb, or at least more numb than usual.

Kerri twitched the contract away, to the side extension of her desk, before racing after Cerb, who fled the building.

"Was that weird?" Pete whispered.

I just rolled my eyes at him. I couldn't say anything that I wanted to, because Kerri came back to her desk. She moved awfully fast, smoothly and silently, despite those high spike-heeled shoes on her feet.

"Sorry about that. I guess we're going to have to keep the door closed from now on, to stop mongrels wandering in." She shrugged and let out a giggle that sounded like wind chimes.

A giggle did not belong in that office, any more than her warm voice belonged with the rest of the impressions I was gathering up about her. Like she was wearing a mask, or maybe even someone was dubbing another person's voice over hers.

My phone rang. Angela.

"Loralee is here, highly agitated, and Maurice says you need to get out of wherever you are," she told me.

Chapter Three

"Yeah, thanks. We were just figuring it out now." I glanced sideways at Pete. "We'll be right there. Sorry about that. I completely forgot we had an appointment."

"This is going to be interesting," Angela said, and hung up.

"You have no idea," I said, smiling as if I thought the person on the other end, who wasn't there anymore, could see me. "See you in five."

I tapped the red button on the phone, as if the connection was still open, and slipped my phone into my pocket. Just in time to stop my keychain from slipping out. Weird. I was always careful to get my keychain deep into my pocket before I got out of my Jeep. Thanks to that scare with the failed carjacker.

"I'm sorry," I told Kerri. "Totally messed up here. We've got an appointment on the other side of town. Could I take the contract with me and read it over and sign it at home, then bring it back tomorrow?"

"Sorry, no can do. We need to have it notarized upon being signed. I'm a notary," she added with another sweet chuckle. Kerri slid the contract into a folder sitting on the far side of her desk and stood up. "When would be convenient for you to come --" She cut herself off with a snarly shriek.

Cerb tore into the office again, as if she hadn't closed the door. Even as I thought that and turned to look, the door swung open, with no one touching it. I swallowed down a bubble of laughter that probably would have sounded half-hysterical if I had let it out. He jumped up onto an empty desk sitting on the other side of the room, then leaped from it to a stack of boxes. They immediately tipped over and flat lawn ornaments on stakes slid out and across the floor. Cerb rode the wave down, his legs going like a hamster in a wheel. Kerri shrieked, and her voice cracked and turned harsh as she lunged across the office. Two men darted in from the back room. They were both dressed all in black and looked somehow dusty and grimy, and just as pale as her. Cerb howled and ran faster, sending lawn ornaments flying in all directions for a few seconds. It looked like a Loony Tunes montage for a few seconds before he skittered down to the floor, got firm footing, and leaped up onto another desk.

Our eyes met, and he gave me a look that very clearly said, *What are you waiting for, stupid?*

I muffled a chuckle and turned to reach for that folder. Pete beat me to it. He grinned and handed me the contract. It stung my fingertips until I shoved it into the pocked on the side of my wheelchair, out of sight. I rubbed my fingers together, and half-expected to find them smoking or maybe red like a couple dozen bees had stabbed them.

"Strategic retreat?" Pete grabbed the handles of my chair to pull me back from Kerri's desk before I could even inhale to respond with an intended, "Heck yeah!"

Cerb darted through the door into the back room, and Kerri and her two henchmen raced after him. There were toppled boxes everywhere and yard decorations on stakes sticking up at all sorts of odd angles that somehow gave a spiky torture chamber look to the front office. The ornaments included the expected flamingos, cows, clowns, frogs, birthday cakes, storks, and some creepy looking black cats, gnomes, leprechauns, and I swear, an entire brigade of Gollums. Hopefully they had a licensing agreement with New Line Cinema and whoever on Peter Jackson's team created that ugly little stinker.

Pete agreed with me. The gnomes and leprechauns looked more creepy than cute. But that was later, on our short drive to Divine's Emporium. We knew better than to say anything until we were safely off that property.

Kerri came running out the door, looking a little frazzled, just as I was climbing into the front seat of the Jeep and Pete was folding up my wheelchair. For just a second, and it was more than just a trick of lighting and shadow, there was something skeletal about her face. Especially the hint of bare teeth and glaring, black eye sockets.

"I'm so sorry," she said, sounding a little breathless. She reached out like she would lean on the door, or maybe try to stop me from closing it. But she stopped with her hand less than an inch away and sort of flinched. Like maybe she felt something she didn't like, or maybe something about my Jeep hurt her.

That might be useful to know. Although looking back later, I decided I didn't want to be in a situation where I would need to use that bit of knowledge.

"We've never had anything happen like that before. Totally inexcusable. I can assure you, we don't run our business like that." She tried to laugh, and brushed some hair out of her face, which had come loose from the immaculate, businesslike chignon.

"Well, I should warn you, since you're setting up business here." I paused to smile and try to read that flicker of something in her eyes. Something dark. Maybe anger? Or apprehension? "This is Neighborlee, the weirdness capital of the state, if not the country. Your realtor should have warned you that odd things happen on a regular basis. Maybe you can get out of the contract if you claim that vital information was withheld." I laughed, and she laughed with me. The sound was brittle and I swear there was an odd sensation of an echo, muffled almost the moment I heard it. "Sorry to take off like that, while you were running around. We really have to get to that appointment before we get in more trouble than we already are."

"Right. Right. So, you'll come back tomorrow? Any time is good. No need to make an appointment. Or you could come back after your appointment, this afternoon."

"Tomorrow is great." I nodded and looked pointedly at my door, to warn her, before I pulled it shut.

"See you tomorrow!" She gave me a chipper smile and backed up a couple steps until she was on the sidewalk in front of the door. Then she loosely wrapped her arms around herself and stood there, watching us, until I put the key in the ignition.

"Oh, wait -- could I see that?" She darted back across the crumbling blacktop, holding out her hand.

I was suddenly very glad the window was rolled up, even though the day was so humid.

"What is that? On your keychain." Her smile widened a little more, and honestly, with the weird vibrations I was getting, I wouldn't have been surprised if her teeth were pointed.

"Just some old beads." I shrugged and turned the key in the ignition.

"Would you mind?" She stopped just short of pressing her hand against the glass.

"Sorry, we're really running late. You can see it tomorrow when we come back."

"That would be great. You ... you wouldn't happen to have any more of those beads, would you?" She chuckled, but the sound had lost its warmth and sounded brittle, and somehow chilly. "I collect beads. Especially unique old ones like those."

"I don't think so." I put the Jeep in reverse, and she finally got the hint and backed away. "See you tomorrow!"

"Tomorrow." Kerri bared her teeth in a thin smile and backed up to the sidewalk of the building. She stood there, watching us, holding onto that smile that made me think of sharks ready to go into a frenzy, until I had backed up and turned and drove out of the parking lot.

Pete watched her in the rearview mirror and didn't move, and maybe didn't even breathe, until we had put the Neighborlee Schools property between us and her.

"We are not going back, are we?" he muttered.

"Our folks didn't raise no dummies."

I took the last possible street to turn left and head for Divine's. Something in me didn't want friendly little Miss Kerri to get the slightest hint of where I was going. If I could have, I would have taken the long way around, but gut instinct was insisting I had to get to Divine's and show that contract to Angela ASAP.

As soon as we turned onto the side street, Pete pulled the contract out of my side bag. From the corner of my eye, I saw him frown as he looked over the first page.

"Something wrong?"

"She let me look at the contract yesterday, and this isn't the same. It starts out the same, but ... this is so weird."

"Weird for normal towns, or weird for Neighborlee?"

"The words are ... they're blurry. Like they really aren't words, just blobs of ink, or maybe it's some new alphabet. But it sure looked like the contract they showed me yesterday, when I took it out of the folder."

I got one of those shivers that started out in the core of my gut and in my scalp, simultaneously, and then the two shivers kind of traveled inward and outward until they met somewhere in my bones and threatened my driving. I admit, I glided through a couple stop signs, more slowing and coasting than actual stopping.

I was alert enough to look for kids at play in front yards or riding bikes in the street. We made it to Divine's without really stopping, and without getting caught by the police or yelled at by angry parents. Then when I put my Jeep in park in front of the gate to Divine's, I held out my hand.

The paper stung my fingers again, and this time there were visible sparks. I nearly dropped the stack. It felt heavier, and thicker, and instead of the staple I saw holding it together, back in the office, now the stack was caught in the corner with an odd-looking binder clip that seemed to have teeth. That wasn't really my imagination, because a closer look showed it had serrated edges where there was normally a rounded edge to a bulldog clip.

Pete was right. The top two-thirds of the top page were in English, proclaiming it to be an employment contract with Pi Surprise Enterprises. The language was pure legalese that threatened to give me a headache. So much repetition and "wherefores" and "except unders" and other language covering every contingency just vaguely enough that a court case to clarify the wording would be more expensive than most plaintiffs could afford. About the two-thirds mark, the words turned blurry, increasing until they outnumbered the readable English words. And the longer I tried to read, the more the paper stung my fingertips.

"It doesn't bother you?" I asked, and paused to blow on my fingertips. They were red. When Pete shook his head, I handed him the stack of papers. "Let's get inside and see what Angela thinks."

He tucked the papers into his back pocket long enough to help me get my chair out. Angela came to the door by this time, and I shivered when I glimpsed her standing in almost the same position I had last seen Kerri, her arms wrapped around herself, as if she were cold.

Cerb came galloping up the sidewalk as I bumped up the curb. He slowed enough to trot circles around us as we turned to go through the gate, then suddenly skidded to a stop and let out a roar that I swear made the sidewalk buckle underneath me.

"What is wrong with him?" I yelped.

Pete turned, walking backward a few steps so he could watch Cerb, and stepped through the gate.

The papers burst into green and black flames. There was a

flash, and a tiny, shrieking voice. Half of one page vanished. The rest turned black with green streaks through them, and gave off a rotten stink that choked me for a moment.

Cerb howled and leaped on Pete, caught the collar of his shirt in his teeth and pulled him back onto the sidewalk. He landed hard and rolled, partially extinguishing the flames.

One more flicker of fire, this time ordinary red and orange flames. Then the fire died entirely. I reached with my hand and my brain, yanking those papers up from where Pete dropped them on the sidewalk. Half the stack was nothing but char that blew away as black dust. The rest darkened and turned to dust in the few seconds it took for Angela to hurry down the path from her door and come through the gate and out onto the sidewalk. Pete was sitting up by this time, and we all watched the dust disintegrate and vanish in the warm afternoon breeze.

"Are you all right?" Angela asked, bending down to Pete and cupping his face in her hands.

"What was that?" I said.

"Some malevolent ... magic, for lack of a better word." She pressed her lips flat and narrowed her eyes and turned unerringly in the general direction of the Pi Surprise building. For just a few heartbeats, I almost felt sorry for the people on the other end of Angela's displeasure.

Almost. They had tried to do something nasty with that contract. That was easy to figure out. What they were trying to do, we could only guess. Worse, they had nearly set my little brother on fire.

That turned out to be more fear than reality. When we got Pete into Divine's and examined him, he was only bruised from landing so hard on the sidewalk. The flames hadn't even singed his jeans or his T-shirt. He had felt heat, but there wasn't any sign of burning on his skin. Angela insisted on washing his clothes, just to make sure nothing inimical clung to them, and gave him soap that smelled of incense, to take a long, hot shower.

By the time Pete came out of the bathroom in Angela's apartment, we were all settled in her living room to have a long discussion and figure out what was going on. Maurice had been busy calming Loralee, who had been frantic, whining and shivering during the three encounters Cerb had with the enemy and their inimical magical attacks. He said he had heard something when the contract burst into flames. That was a little frightening, because he had been inside the shop when it happened.

"Near as I can come, it was like a huge cloud of buzzard-sized mosquitos, shrieking in fury and then terror and then ..." He chuckled as he settled down on the table, where Angela had put a doll-sized table and chair and a tiny cup the size of his head, filled with her special spicy-sweet purple tea. "Heck if it didn't sound like a villain in a bad comedy, who shouts, 'No, this can't be happening, I'm invincible,' just before he breaks into a thousand pieces or blows up or something."

"I'm glad you can find some amusement in all this." Angela straightened up from putting down two large mixing bowls on the floor, so Cerb and Loralee could share in the restorative tea.

Diane was working downstairs with Meggie, so Angela didn't have to worry about the counter and any customers who might come in during our meeting. I had the sneaking suspicion that if Pete had known Meggie was there, he would have played the idiotic hero and insisted that no, he was fine, there was no need to wash his clothes and take a shower. And then he would have stayed at the shop the entire afternoon, hoping for some praise and hero worship.

"So ya think it's a good thing we didn't sign the contract?" Pete said, coming out of the bathroom. He was wearing an exact replica of Mal Reynolds' costume from *Firefly*, minus the suspenders and duster and gun. I could almost laugh, and I was grateful to Angela for knowing just what would please Pete. He had already loved that show long before he found out Meggie loved it too. I had lost count of how many times he talked about how they had been friends in the online fan group, The Browncoats, before they met in person.

Yet I had to wonder, for a few disturbing seconds: did Angela dig out the costume for him to raise his spirits, because this afternoon's close call had been far too close?

"Yes, it's a very good thing." Angela settled at the table, reached for the last empty mug, and filled it for Pete. "When someone goes to so much trouble to disguise their intent with illusion so that it stinks badly enough for Cerb to smell and come running, then there definitely is something dangerous involved."

"Wish we could have gotten a good look at the wording," Maurice said.

Angela had to repeat his words for Pete. He couldn't hear or see Maurice any more than Meggie could.

"What if it's like those stories we were reading in English class last fall?" Pete mused. He sighed but obeyed when Angela gestured for him to drink. "The ones where people got tricked into signing their souls away to the devil," he continued, after taking several large gulps big enough to make his Adam's apple bob. My throat hurt in sympathy.

"I'm especially worried that they needed you, Lanie, to sign the contract," Angela said.

"What about the other boys who came to sign when we were there?" I said.

We spent the afternoon making phone calls and trying to figure out what to do next. I called Gordon and then Kurt. I asked Gordon if he could check on the background of the Pi Surprise people, their business licenses and lease agreement. Then I asked Kurt to swing by the building and try to use his particular gift to get a good reading on the place and the people.

Pete called the two boys to ask them about the contracts they had signed. They told him their contracts had only been one sheet of paper, printed front and back. The terms were simple. Maybe frighteningly simple and clear. They agreed they were outside contractors with Pi Surprise. They didn't expect any insurance or retirement benefits. They wouldn't sue the company if they were hurt while performing their duties, and either side could cancel employment at any time without repercussions or requiring explanation.

At least, they *thought* they had signed a contract that was simple and took up only one sheet of paper. We knew better than to even hint to them that they saw one thing and signed another.

The alternative to the boys having been fooled by an illusion, and maybe signing away their souls ... was that only Pete and I had been given that strange, nearly lethal, incendiary contract. And that raised all sorts of options that threatened to generate a massive headache.

The question of when Kerri would realize we had taken the contract hung over our heads for the rest of the day.

Kurt called just before dinner. He had swung by the Pi building on his way back from an installation and troubleshooting job that took him to Columbus. Just to check out his sense of energy at work. He wasn't about to go in, or get close enough for those people to see and target him.

There was no one in the building. Two windows were broken and covered with plywood sheeting. The long plastic banner wasn't there. Neither was the sign that Pete had seen, about hiring. A small, neon orange sign hung in its place, stating the building was condemned. It was faded in streaks from long exposure to the sun.

Gordon got back to us the next day to report that no applications for business permits and licenses had been filed. Not for use of the building, not for Pi Surprise operating in Neighborlee, or Cuyahoga County. There was no business named Pi Surprise at the location listed on the flyers they had been passing out in town for weeks. Honestly, I was somewhat surprised that the flyer Pete had kept hadn't disintegrated or turned to ashes at the same time as the contract. Plus, a little further digging located the realtor that held the contract for leasing the former flower market. She said no one had inquired about the building for more than four months. The last person who did was only interested in the land the building sat on. He didn't want to be responsible for the environmental impact studies and the expense of tearing down the building to clear the land for new development.

In the end, it really didn't matter what destroyed the illusion. Kerri and her minions had fled. Did the exact reason and timing matter? When they realized Pete and I had taken the contract? Or did they feel the destruction of the contract coming up against the protective magic enclosing Divine's? Pi Surprise was gone. All of us held our breaths for a few days, waiting for news. What were the chances those three would show up in a hospital or be found unconscious in a field somewhere, with a huge blank spot in their memories? Either they were willing minions, or they had been used like puppets by some malevolent force.

Then as a topper to all the ugly weirdness piling up on us, Harry brought up something I noticed, but didn't consciously register. The men working with Kerri were also pale and dressed all in black. Long sleeves and long pants. Despite the heat of the day.

The guy who tried to steal my Jeep: pale in skin and hair, dressed all in black.

Maybe he worked with them?

So when Kerri asked to see my keychain, was she trying to steal my Jeep? Why?

The other alternative was even more disturbing, because it raised so many questions.

"She was interested in the beads," Pete agreed with me, after we sat around, dissecting the few facts we had and all the warped possibilities.

"What's so special about them?" Harry asked.

"You mean besides Emma making jewelry out of them?" I reached out with a thought and yanked my keys out of my backpack from across the kitchen, and brought them over to me. "Pete, how many do you have left from that bag of beads your mom got?"

He thought for a few moments, frowning, then shrugged. He was only six when his parents were killed.

We ended up ransacking all those crates of files and diaries and paperwork Col. Hayward's people had removed from the farmhouse, back when our parents first disappeared in Bermuda. They had kept most of the papers from all the research Pete's parents had been doing when they were killed. If there was anything to find out after all these years about those beads, they would be in Emma's diary.

Too bad I couldn't remember anything unusual about either the secondhand shop where Emma found the beads, or if anything unusual happened after she bought them. After all, Mum and I had been there with her. I didn't sense anything when I held the bag, carrying it for her until we got to the register. Nothing bizarre happened during the remainder of our visit with the Crowders. Nothing unusual occurred when Mum wore the bracelet and earrings Emma made for her. Nothing bizarre about the little thong bracelet Jake had made for Pete, or my keychain.

Until now.

What had happened to activate the interest of Kerri and her minions, and just how much trouble were we in?

The banker's boxes and plastic storage bins were in my attic, so Pete and Harry had to climb up to get them. We found the notation about Emma spending the day with us and hitting several secondhand shops in Cornwall. Notes about the earrings and bracelet made for Mum. The earrings were in my jewelry box, and Mum had taken the bracelet to Bermuda. Pete still wore the leather bracelet Jake had made for him. He never took it off except for showers, and when the leather thong wore out and had to be replaced. In fact, just about a month ago, Pete had dug out that bag of beads to make a bracelet for Meggie, when they started getting serious about each other.

"You know," Harry said, "if the carjacker was after the beads and not the keys, and that woman wanted to look at the beads ... what are the chances they'll come here, looking for them?"

"Why are they suddenly interested after all these years?" Pete said.

"Maybe because you haven't done anything with them until you made Meggie's bracelet." I felt a brief wave of nausea. "Oh. Heck. Meggie."

Pete nearly knocked himself out of his chair at the table, he was in that much a hurry to pull out his phone and call her, to warn her.

"Maybe we should get the beads out of the house?" Harry muttered, as Pete left a message on Meggie's voicemail.

"Well, there's no safer place to store them than Divine's," I said. "Maybe Angela will know what's up with them."

"What if the beads burn up when we try to take them past the fence?"

I was stuck, trying to come up with a smart-aleck response. The mildest one was: *Good! Problem solved.* We listened to Pete finishing his stumbling message for Meggie. Fortunately, she had enough experience with the magic of Divine's, starting with her brother Troy's trip through a painting with Diane Rittenhouse, she would believe him when Pete said the beads might be dangerous.

Then Loralee and Cerb came into the house, from wherever they had been patrolling for the day. Loralee sneezed. Loud and hard. Cerb froze and his tail stuck out stiff and straight. It might have been funny, except he was very visibly worried for Loralee. She sneezed again. Hard enough to push her back a few steps, sliding on the tile floor. With purple sparks swirling around her head for a few seconds. Cerb whined.

Loralee went up on her hind legs and rested her front paws on the table and zeroed in on the beads -- keychain, thong bracelet, earrings, and bag of unused beads -- spread out on the placemats in the center. She shook her head, and her eyes watered and she sneezed hard enough to push her back again.

Cerb let out a whining sort of growl and looked at me.

"We're getting them out of the house right now," I promised him, and reached for the bag. Pete picked up the placemat and bent it into a funnel, to slide the beads into the bag.

Harry had the idea for Cerb to run ahead to Divine's, to tell Maurice what happened, so Angela could be ready for us.

"Problem," he said, when we were on our way, in my Jeep. "How come Loralee hasn't been allergic to your keychain or Pete's bracelet?"

Chapter Four

"Quantity, I have to assume," Angela said, when we presented her with the bag of beads and our questions. "Exposure to daylight, perhaps. And perhaps the variations in the designs embedded in the beads have something to do with it. I am sensing a slight vibration. Not a sound, not any kind of energy I have ever encountered before. So very faint … I'm sorry, there isn't enough for me to even guess the purpose of the beads, the source of the energy running through them, or how they work."

"Can you muffle it so the creeps can't track it here? Put it in storage with all the other dangerous stuff you've got locked away?" I asked.

"Of course." She hefted the bag of beads, studying it with narrowed eyes. "I have a box that should do very nicely, silencing whatever the effect is. And I'll do one step better. I'm going to put in a call to an archeologist friend. It might take months for him to respond, with the time differential … We'll have an answer for you, eventually."

I dismembered my keychain to leave those beads with Angela, and Pete left his bracelet. I felt kind of bad for him. He just didn't have much left of anything to remind him of his parents. Of course, we completely forgot about the earrings until then. When Pete got the beads back from Meggie, I would bring them and the earrings and add them to the safe storage at Divine's.

This was something else to add to the growing list of details about Pi Surprise and the deepening "huh?" factor surrounding the whole incident. We brought the rest of the guardians in on the questions, and spent that Sunday afternoon relaxing at Felicity and Jake's place, barbecuing and theorizing.

The thing was, the more we went through all the details of the weird episode, the more sure we were it didn't have the same feel as when we had faced attacks and infiltration attempts by the Rivals. This was more along the lines of my freshman year of college, that creepy house on the border of Darbyville, the wishing box, and the incident with the time travel watch. Maybe this was someone new in the battle? Not a good theory. We had been enjoying the quiet respite after the Rivals tripped themselves up so badly last fall.

If this enemy was unrelated to either Big Ugly or the Rivals, maybe they weren't someone new, but a foe who had retreated after that battle? Someone who had returned for another try? If this was a testing foray, in preparation for a renewed attack, or just a blip on the radar, we wouldn't know until we examined everything in hindsight.

Thinking of the time travel watch and the Time Lords, I decided to have a talk with the twins, Rodney and Rita Shipton. Just to ask them to be extra alert. One thing we had learned through experience: odd events never happened alone. They came in groups, sometimes a trickle, sometimes a tidal wave.

After Rodney's and Rita's extended brush with the general weirdness of Neighborlee, they had settled in and become part of the town. They didn't have any special gifts to make them guardians, but they were like Charlotte Longfellow -- they were support staff. When they graduated from Willis-Brooks, they had stayed. Rodney worked security on campus and Rita became a dorm supervisor. At our old dorm, Wickslow Hall. Both of them kept their eyes open for signs of weirdness affecting the students. They made a point of steering new students to Divine's Emporium, to have them tested by Angela. She let the twins know if anyone needed special handling.

I decided to wait until the end of the week, when we had our monthly Trek club meeting, to talk to the twins. I had other concerns on my mind.

Loralee was sleep-digging. She got out of the nest she and Cerb had made in Harry's old room and meandered around until the fabric of the wall or the floor parted for her and let her walk straight out into the yard. Then she dug. With her eyes closed.

The holes started appearing in my yard the day after Loralee sneezed. Allergic reaction? Who could be sure, since her dog shape wasn't her normal form? I suspected her or Cerb, but wasn't quite sure what to say. Face it, accusing my magical anthropomorphic houseguests of digging foot-deep holes in my backyard, conveniently placed for someone to break an ankle or worse, was kind of rude when I had no proof.

After the third morning waking up to find a new hole in the side yard between the driveway and fence, I decided to get help. I asked Kurt to set up a camera system with motion detectors, to catch whoever or whatever was turning my yard into a moonscape. He teased me that I really didn't want to stop the culprit. If this kept up, I wouldn't have any grass in my yard, so I wouldn't have to mow for the entire summer and maybe into the fall.

That night, the cameras caught Loralee coming out through the wall and kind of floating down a couple feet to the grass. Her eyes were closed and she sniffed around until she came to a spot next to the foundation of the garage apartment. She dug until she tossed something behind her onto the pile of dirt. Not once did her eyes open, not even when she turned around and walked back to the house and through the wall.

Kurt woke up just before 5am, checked the camera feed that went to his workshop, and called me by 5:05. By the time he got to my house, Pete and I had watched the video feed on my computer, and were outside, staring at what Loralee had dug up. This evidence of the strength in those tiny paws of hers made me doubly reluctant to confront her about the holes in the yard.

She had brought up a skull. Not a mouse or squirrel or rabbit. Human.

I called Gordon, who arrived about five minutes after Kurt pulled into the driveway. The two of them stood there on the edge of the pile of dirt, just shaking their heads, neither one of them able to come up with any smart-aleck remarks. After maybe ten minutes of the four of us alternating between looking at the skull and looking at each other, Gordon shrugged and headed back to his truck to get his kit and call it in.

"Where there's a skull ..." Kurt didn't finish saying what we were all thinking. He sidestepped the dirt to look down into the hole Loralee had dug.

About then, we decided to wake up Harry. Just in case the police needed to dig down into the foundation of his apartment. The four of us went back into my place and I wheeled down the hall to Cerb and Loralee's room. They were both asleep. She didn't even have any dirt on her. I felt kind of stupid, explaining to them what happened, because I didn't get any reaction from either of them. Not even a little panting or a tongue hanging out of the mouth. Just big-eyed focus on me. Then when I finished, Cerb nuzzled Loralee, turned, kind of twisted sideways, and vanished. I shouldn't have been as surprised by it as I was, because I had just seen the video of Loralee doing the same thing several hours earlier.

Angela called while Harry was finishing making breakfast for us. She was on her way over, because Maurice needed to speak with me. The terms of his exile on Earth meant he couldn't take interdimensional shortcuts like Cerb could, so he had to fly or walk or ride with or on someone, when he wanted to get anywhere. While she was telling me all this, Cerb reappeared. He and Loralee settled down on the blankets by the back door, to wait for breakfast and just watch us.

By the time Angela arrived, the coroner had come, along with the detectives who handled homicide, and Chief Tanner. Gordon set up crime scene tape around the hole and knocked on the door to ask Kurt to email the video file to his tablet. Maurice was riding on Angela's shoulder. By the time we finished our delayed breakfast and figured out what was going on, Maurice and I were both a little irritated by the limitations imposed on us by differing levels of sensitivity to magic. Only Angela, Kurt, and I could see or hear Maurice, and only Maurice and Angela could talk to Cerb and Loralee. It led to lots of duplicated conversation, having to repeat for the boys whatever Maurice told us.

The worst part? The explanation.

Apparently, living in a physical form that wasn't her original shape, and then all the complications of being pregnant, did strange things to Loralee's magic and her control over her shape. The sneezing fit brought on by the beads had knocked things out of whack, to put it simply. The dog aspect took over when she was most deeply asleep. That wasn't the bizarre part. The really strange part of the explanation was that Loralee was having cravings, but they were manifesting as a need to dig, instead of weird obsessive tastes in food.

So what could we do about it?

Basically, nothing. We couldn't put a leash on Loralee to keep her in one place, because she was doing it in her sleep, sliding between the molecules in the fabric of space and time to get outside. Angela suggested that Loralee and Cerb come stay at Divine's Emporium, and she would dial down the defensive magic of the shop until the frequencies no longer irritated the expectant mother.

While that suggestion made sense, it was a no-go.

Another fun surprise: Loralee had imprinted on my house. Apparently the nesting or denning urge, or whatever the proper name was for the instinct to settle in and get comfy before giving birth, had *bonded* her to my house. Moving her to Divine's, even if the atmosphere adjusted until it helped her pregnancy, wouldn't do her any good. Chances were, as soon as she went to sleep, she would walk through walls and cross streets and neighborhoods to get back to my house.

Chief Tanner's interruption, coming in to talk with us, satisfy his curiosity about all the holes in my yard, and get a cup of coffee, was more than welcome. We didn't have coffee, but we did offer him Pop's special blend of tea, and Angela provided the explanation: I was looking after the pregnant dog of a friend who was out of town. He didn't even blink when we admitted we weren't sure how Loralee got out of the house every night to dig. We knew better than to admit she was digging in her sleep.

The police dug under the foundation of the garage several feet, looking for more bones that went with the skull. On the plus side, we had visible proof that whoever built my house did a great job, creating a nice, thick slab of concrete for the pad for the garage. The negative side … well, there were several.

The diggers found four mangled and chewed up gnome lawn decorations. They weren't the usual garden gnomes with the big, pointed hats. They were Pi Surprise style gnomes. I almost felt sorry for them until I had to wonder what had been going on that they were so chewed up, cracked and even melted in spots. Like they had been in a battle. How had they been buried under the foundation of my garage-turned-apartment? Who had destroyed them? What kind of fight had they been in? And even creepier: how could lawn decorations get into a fight to begin with? Maybe they were being used like probes by Pi Surprise, to spy on the house and find the location of the beads and … what? They got yanked through holes in space and time, the same way Loralee and Cerb slipped in and out through the walls of the house?

I was getting a headache speculating on all the possibilities. And seriously, what was the use of doing that to myself, when we couldn't get any solid answers?

The other negative result from that morning was that no more bones came to light before the miniscule crime investigation team of Neighborlee PD packed up and left. They weren't exactly certain how to proceed from there, short of digging up my entire yard and maybe destroying the garage foundation in search of those bones. We agreed that they wouldn't come back and hunt any further until after some work had been done identifying the skull.

All that excitement occurred in just two hours before I headed to work. Since I worked at a newspaper, everyone was interested and talking about the discovery in my back yard. I couldn't get away from the odd incident.

Naturally, since we were watching for Loralee to dig again, she didn't dig for two more nights.

The third night, she dug in my front yard. Bryce Lucking, another friend, was driving through on patrol in our neighborhood that night. When he saw the little white shape in the middle of my yard, he parked and pulled out his night vision goggles and settled down to watch. Those goggles were not standard Neighborlee PD issue. Bryce was a geek who loved his techno toys, so he was allowed to bring them when he was on patrol. Especially at night.

He also put the whole thing on his dash cam, so there was nothing we could do for damage control when Loralee dug up emeralds and pearls the size of robins' eggs and scattered them across the pile of dirt. Bryce saw them. He took pictures with his cell phone and called in the report. Then he sat there, keeping watch on the handful of gems, called me on the phone and woke me up, at 4 in the morning. He wasn't about to touch anything, and he knew better than to break the chain of custody when it came to highly suspicious items. Gems of that size, found in a hole less than a foot deep, qualified as suspicious.

We would have liked to have kept the entire incident quiet, but procedure required the Chief notify authorities in the FBI, to find out about any stolen jewels that matched the description of what had been found in my front yard. There were leaks somewhere in the bureau, because by 6 that evening, we had reporters from newspapers, TV and radio stations clamoring for further information, the "inside scoop." Daniel intervened and told anybody who was part of the Sheridan Communications empire to leave me alone. I appreciated that. Unfortunately, he could only ask, not give direct orders, when it came to local stations and affiliates of the major networks. Asking for that courtesy just stirred things up, making people wonder what inside information he had. Any attempt to "kill" the story just made some of those reporters more sure something sensational was going on, and they were determined not to be left behind.

Friday evening, I came home from work just in time to see a total stranger pull his truck up onto my lawn, next to the filled-in hole. He stepped out, reached into the open bed of his truck, and pulled out a post hole digger. Then he jammed it into the ground about two feet from the hole. He had the gall to yell at me to go away, when I pulled into my own driveway. He said he had permission from the owner to dig and I was trying to jump his claim.

"No, you're trespassing and damaging private property, on top of being a bald-faced liar," I shot back, before I even opened the door to get out of my Jeep. I was furious and had a headache from fielding too many phone calls at work about the gems, and feeling guilty about the ruckus at the office.

"Who you calling a liar?" he snarled at me, and slung that post hole digger over his massive shoulder like a cave man would sling a club, before stomping over to face me down.

"You are, because you do not have permission from the owner." I had my cell phone in my pocket, because I had had another one of those phone calls on the way home. How did the creep get my unlisted cell phone number? That just made me angrier. So now I pulled the phone out and waved it at him. "You've got two seconds to get off my front lawn."

He cussed me out, adding, "Do so have permission from the owner!"

"I'm the owner, you fewmets-for-brains. And you just used up more than your two seconds."

"Now hold on there, don't you go making any stupid mistakes. You're not going to call the police."

"You bet I am." Then I shoved him hard with my brain.

Sometimes it's good to be a semi-pseudo-superhero.

Even if I did nearly give myself a nosebleed from the effort.

He stumbled backwards, flailing to catch hold of that post hole digger. And, oh, what a pity, he ended up slamming it into the window of his truck. That shatter-proof glass didn't break, but it made a lovely spiderweb pattern that filled the entire frame. There was no way he was driving because he couldn't possibly see through that obstruction.

I pressed the speed dial for Gordon. It paid to have a good friend who was not only a cop, but knew how to look intimidating just by standing up straight and scowling.

The guy was so busy cussing and regaining his feet, I had time to get my back door open and swing my wheelchair out. I needed to sit down before my legs folded up and I ended up on the ground. Not a good position for confronting a lying bozo would-be prospector with a mouth like a sewer. He slammed the post hole digger back into his truck, punctuated with a dozen more curses, and finally turned around to look at me. He stopped in the middle of telling me I'd pay big-time for lying to the cops. He swallowed loudly, hard enough I could see his adam's apple bob from ten feet away. He looked at my wheelchair. He went pale, then went bright red, and started in on cussing me out. Like somehow I was violating his rights by being in a wheelchair.

About that time, Mercedes and Joe and Charlene, my closest neighbors on the street, had either come home from work or had been drawn outside by the noise. Charlene was a tiny little gray-haired lady who reminded me of a sparrow. She had a voice like a foghorn and the lung power and attitude to match an ice breaker on the Arctic Ocean. She stomped up to the treasure hunter and had to jump up to slap his filthy mouth. She also had a good right hook that would make George Foreman green with jealousy. The guy stumbled backwards, banged his head against his truck, and kind of slumped down on the ground. He gaped like a fish for a few seconds while she tore into him, scolding him for his language and for giving "poor little Lanie" a hard time.

Gordon and Mandy drove up before the treasure hunter could do more than get onto his knees and try to pull himself upright. They were in his patrol SUV, because Mandy was riding with me to our club meeting. Gordon wasn't getting off work until the meeting was half over, so he would meet her there at the community arts building where we were meeting. The treasure hunter's face screwed up like he was going to burst into tears, then he turned to look at me.

"I told you not to call the police. What'd you go and do that for?" he whined.

"Gee, maybe because you were threatening me in my own front yard?" I shot back.

"Lying --" He got out several epithets that implied he had the constitutional right to denigrate me simply because I was female. Charlene slapped him hard again, banging his head against the truck.

Poor Gordon was fighting so hard not to burst out laughing. Mandy just shook her head and strolled over to stand with me.

Gordon had to take the treasure hunter to the hospital to get two stitches in the back of his head before booking him. Yeah, I was pressing charges. The guy finally shut up after Gordon told him for the fifth time that yes, that "deleted-expletive useless excuse for a female" was indeed the property owner.

On the way to the hospital, Gordon worked his magic and got the guy to turn off the filth and threats long enough to get some actual facts from him to put in his report. He found out the treasure hunter had stopped at my parents' farmhouse to dig, first. The people renting the farmhouse were on their way out the door and stopped him from digging. They thought it was funny that the guy came to the wrong Zephyr property to dig. They not only gave him my address, and directions how to get there, but they claimed they were the owners of my house, and I was the renter. They gave the treasure hunter permission to dig, and advice on how to deal with the delusional drug addict who was living in the house.

Those renters had been a headache to deal with for the last four months, to the point that Kurt insisted on collecting the rent for me. When Gordon called to tell me what further trouble they had caused, that just doubled my determination to find a way to break the leasing agreement. Maybe now I finally had enough legal justification to send them packing. They told the treasure hunter I was desperate for money and wouldn't hesitate to offer some entertainment for the evening, once he was done digging. That explained some of the things the treasure hunter said to me. He had already been primed to think I was a desperate, kinky hooker. Seeing me in the wheelchair must have really thrown him off balance. I don't know why, but a lot of people equate physical handicap with some sort of communicable disease.

Gordon had the recorder on in his patrol car, so the whole story was saved in the police records. He told me if I didn't start eviction procedures on the renters, he would do it for me.

Harry and Pete had both come home just before Gordon called. I put Gordon on speaker phone, so I wouldn't have to repeat anything. As a result, my brothers wanted to head out to the farmhouse right away, to toss the renters out into the street. We couldn't do that without following legal procedures. Besides, I had a club meeting to run in another twenty minutes. Gordon promised he would swing by the farm once he had put the treasure hunter into official custody. He needed to talk with the renters to get their side of the story anyway. If I knew Gordon, he would let those people know how disappointed he was by the nasty trick they had pulled. Maybe he would encourage them, politely, to end the lease ASAP and get out of Neighborlee, ASAP.

So, Pete and Mandy and I headed out to the meeting, with a side trip to Divine's to pick up Maurice. We had to swing by Hunky & Dory's for sandwiches, since I certainly didn't have time to throw dinner together. Harry planned to spend the evening with his car parked across the front lawn, and sitting guard on the back yard. Just in case more idiots with no grasp of the concept of private property decided to do some treasure hunting.

Was it any wonder, after all that excitement, I nearly forgot to ask Rodney and Rita to keep an eye out for weirdness, as the first summer term was ending at Willis-Brooks College?

As it turned out, Harry was smart to stay home and keep watch. He was in the back yard, treating himself, Loralee, and Cerb to some barbecue, when he heard car doors open and slam closed, and people raising their voices in complaint. He wandered down the driveway to the front and saw two cars parked in front of my house in the street, and a half-dozen people walking around his car, which was taking up maybe two-thirds of the front yard. Harry waited until he heard them talking about trying to raise his car up on their jacks, to make enough room for them to start digging underneath it. He took pictures of their cars and of them before they noticed him. He lied and told them he had gotten all their plotting on voice recorder on his phone, and he had just called the police. Two of the guys ran for one car. The other four guys headed for Harry, starting to cuss him out. Why is foul language always the first recourse of people who are very clearly in the wrong?

Then Cerb tore around the side of the house, three times his normal size, eyes red with fury, growling, flashing his fangs and foaming at the mouth. The four guys ran each other over and knocked themselves off their own feet a few times as they scrambled to get to their car.

Harry was still laughing when he strolled back down the driveway to the backyard and discovered two kids who had showed up while he was gone. They probably weren't out of elementary school yet, and were digging in the back yard under the sleepy gaze of Loralee, using sand pails and shovels. Harry knew them, because they lived just down the street from us, around the corner. He called their parents, then he asked our neighbors if they would mind parking their cars on my front lawn to entirely block it, so he could park his car on the grass in the back yard. Then he called the police to report what had happened.

He ended up spending a couple hours down at the station. It turned out the foursome Cerb had scared were so badly frightened, they drove like they were drunks. Doing forty-five in a twenty-five zone, they sideswiped the brick pillars at the end of someone's driveway. Harry was a witness and had to verify what those outsiders were doing in a quiet residential section of Neighborlee on a balmy summer evening.

Gordon showed up later than usual at the arts center to join our Trek club meeting. He had gone out to our parents' home to confront the renters and get their side of the story. He found no cars in the driveway, but lots of suspicious holes dug in the backyard. While he was walking around, taking pictures, the renters returned from a week-long stay with the wife's aunt, who had fallen and broken her hip. They were upset when Gordon asked for proof that they had been away from the house for the whole week, but were able to produce receipts from when they stopped for gas and food on the way back from Memphis. Their irritation dissipated when they saw the holes dug in the backyard and evidence that someone had tried to break into the house. Gordon, being Gordon, wrote up a report on the attempted break-in, verified nothing of their property had been stolen, then had a word with them about the consistently late rent payments. My hero.

~~~~~
~~~~~

Pete and I were late getting home that night, because Rita and Rodney needed to talk privately with me, about some growing concerns of their own. Five summer term students in Rita's dorm were involved in a life sciences project. They were going to be seniors in the fall, and they were working on a project they had designed themselves: an intensive study of the eco-system of Black Water Pool.

I got chills as soon as I heard those three words. Black Water Pool had been quiet, perhaps too quiet, since that Senior Prank Night when Kurt, Felicity and I had foiled Reggie Grandstone's plot to blow up the rock wall of Black Water Pool. The intent had been to empty it, destroying Pickle Falls in the process, just so Reggie and his brother Freddie and their idiot henchmen could ride stolen rafts and canoes down the flooded river. We had managed to defuse and then drop pallets of homemade fertilizer bombs into the pool. At least, we hoped we had defused the bombs. For all we knew, the bombs had gone off, deep under the surface, and we had yet to encounter the results.

The life sciences teacher who had given the students permission to do the study was relatively new to Neighborlee, so maybe he could be excused. Yet at the same time, his department head should have thrown up a red flag and done something to either veto or change the project. Dr. Schwitzfield was a long-time Neighborlee resident, so he knew the stories about Black Water, the legends and rumors. He knew how people who messed with the odd elements of Neighborlee never prospered. He should have said or done something.

Chapter Five

It had taken the last two weeks for Rita and Rodney to find out who knew what, who had approved or tried to stop the research project, any questions or unusual interest in the project and those involved, and what the responses had been. They were also waiting to see if the students had been showing any reaction to exposure to the otherness in the air and water. So far, the students didn't seem to be showing any effects, either negative or positive.

Two students were experienced scuba divers. They went down the steep sides of the pool to gather up samples of the silt and water plants, and catch fish and bugs living in the water. Others in the team were sampling and testing the wildlife living on the rim of the pool. A third team, experienced rock climbers, were investigating the sides of Pickle Falls, getting samples of the lichen that clung to the rocks, the vines, and the other plants that lived partially hidden by the spray of falling water.

It sounded all very scientific and labor-intensive, and honestly, kind of boring. At least, boring for anyone who wasn't a resident of Neighborlee and didn't know the history of the pool and the falls. It was no consolation to know that park rangers regularly stopped to watch the students at work and check their equipment and safety procedures.

I got a deeper chill when Rita said she and Rodney had been so focused on the life sciences students, she hadn't noticed something odd happening on third floor. Our floor, our freshman year at WB. Specifically, something odd about the phone booth. She couldn't put her finger on it, other than seeing odd shimmers of light reflecting off the glass panels of the door, during the day. The phone booth was near the middle of the floor, always in shadow when the ceiling lights were off, and too far from the windows on either end of the floor for any natural daylight to reach it.

Years ago, when the dorms were being renovated and redecorated, someone had decided to be whimsical and install real phone booths in the dorm for the on-campus phones. For a few months after the big explosion of inimical magic in our freshman year, I had thought I heard whispers and sounds that shouldn't have been on our floor. Not very often. Not very loud. Just hazy enough and always late enough at night, I couldn't be sure I hadn't really overheard someone's TV or stereo, or maybe I was still dreaming when I got up to scurry down the hall to the bathroom.

Now, though, Rita had heard men's voices when she was on the floor all by herself, during the day. Two days ago, she thought she saw a reflection of an old-style car in one of the glass panels of the phone booth door. With the ruckus over the discovery of the jewels in my front yard, she had hesitated to call me. She and Rodney had agreed to wait until the club meeting to talk privately about the dorm weirdness. They were both very careful about drawing attention to themselves, when it came to handling the weirdness of Neighborlee. Or maybe they just didn't want to be seen talking to me too often? I didn't blame them. Sometimes I felt like the guardians had targets painted on our foreheads.

I was grateful for their alertness, and I was irritated, and I really wished they had gone to Angela instead of me. Or Kurt. It wasn't like they didn't know Kurt. He had played a big part in straightening out the problem with the time traveling watch that nearly destroyed their school careers before they even got started.

We agreed that I would come visit the dorm. They left it to me to call Kurt and have him stop in during open dorm hours, and use his particular gift as a guardian, to assess the situation. Pete suggested that maybe we should bring in Maurice and ask for his view of things. After all, his two years of exile on Earth required him to learn to be useful and help others with their problems. This qualified as a problem, didn't it?

~~~~~

Painfully early the next morning, Loralee dug two holes. One had hip bones. The other had rubies and sapphires. This time I called Chief Tanner, instead of Gordon. He had had a long shift the day before and had gone above and beyond trying to help sort out the mess with the treasure hunter and the unpleasant renters. The Chief brought the part-time CSI guys, who took pictures and soil samples and carefully documented everything found in the holes. Then they took everything with them for identification.

The Chief pointed out something that had escaped us, among all the other weirdness of the whole situation. Everything in the
~~~~~

holes our mommy-to-be had dug up was clean. Nothing looked like it had been buried for even a few hours, let alone years. He could tell from the texture of the grass and the thickness of the compacted dirt in the lawn surrounding the holes, nothing had been disturbed for years. He thought he was funny when he gave me a lecture on proper lawn maintenance, including aerating. Yeah, like I needed that right about now?

Plus, we had the security camera footage, proving Loralee had gone out, dug the holes, and when she stepped away the jewels and bones were in there. No way she could have walked away, someone stopped the cameras, rewound the footage, inserted the bones and jewels, and then placed her just right to get a seamless transition from one section of the video to the next.

There was no way I could tell him Loralee wasn't a dog in her natural form, and the things appearing in the holes were magic spilling over from one dimension to the next.

"Big mistake. You shouldn't have let that stuff out of your hands," Maurice said, when I stopped in at Divine's later that morning to update him and Angela.

"Why?" I got a shiver, despite my irritation at the mischief sparkling in his eyes.

"Faerie gold," Angela said with a sigh.

We were sitting on the front porch. She had been blowing multi-colored soap bubbles and creating animal figures when I pulled up and got out of my Jeep. For punctuation, she blew a bubble that enclosed Maurice and spun him around in the air a few times before it popped. He fluttered his wings extra hard, getting rid of a few droplets, and dropped down to sit on my knee.

"Yeah, essentially faerie gold. The stuff isn't really jewels any more than Lora and Cerb are dogs. There's an energy field around your place, just because of you living there and stuff soaking in. That's not a really good explanation, but you don't need a lesson in Fae physics right now, do you?" He shook his head and continued, without waiting for me to respond. "So when that stuff pops in from another dimension, in reaction to all the blips of pregnancy magic Lora's giving off … it takes on some physical form, but it needs to stay within the field you've built up in your house for it to *stay* jewels and bones and whatever."

"Oh, great." I closed my eyes and really wished I had stayed in bed a couple hours longer. Hard to do when the alarm going off before dawn warned us that Loralee had been digging again and leaving us more trouble-causing presents. "How long until everything in police custody starts to change?"

"Oh, they won't change. Not like faerie gold would turn into leaves or whatever in the old stories. Those were usually illusion, to punish someone who tried to trick the Fae back in the old days. These will just evaporate. Turn back to energy and filter away." Maurice shrugged. "Problem solved."

"Yeah, until someone raises the alarm because the bones they're trying to identify, for a possible murder victim, just vanished out of a locked drawer in the forensics lab. It's not like we can break in and steal the stuff. That'd just cause more trouble." Then a thought occurred to me.

Angela laughed. She winked at me and nodded at Maurice, and I knew she had guessed what I was thinking.

"How good are you at going through walls, phasing in and out, and how much stuff can you carry with you when you do?" I asked.

"Huh? You're asking me to pull off a robbery?" Maurice tried to look piously offended at the idea. He failed, and laughed. "Nobody would ever catch me on security cameras, that's for sure."

"That you know of," Angela said. "If children can see you in your current form, maybe electronics can, too."

"Oh, great. I've been horsing around, giving some people a hard … umm, you didn't hear me just say that." Maurice flicked his wings hard, shooting up a few feet over our heads.

"What have you been doing that you think you were caught on security cameras?" I had to ask.

"Nothing. Nothing." A shrug. A grin. "Nothing much. I just followed a couple jerk tourists the other week, after they tried to talk Angela into giving them a discount on some of that antique glass they kept insisting was junk. They went to that ATM over on Orchard and I kind of bounced around on the keypad, messing up their security code a couple times, then kept changing the amount of money they wanted to withdraw."

"Oh, Maurice …" Angela sighed, but the same mischief sparkled in her eyes. "Thank you. Those people were especially irritating. They kept trying to change price stickers even after I caught them. I was hard pressed not to call the police for a friendly little citizen's report, to get them stopped before they left the city limits. Just to scare them a little."

"Creeps like that don't scare easily," I had to say.

We discussed the options of how to deal with future treasure hunters trying to dig in my yard, and how long this current phase of Loralee's pregnancy cravings would last. One option was to let the intruders keep whatever they found. We could entertain ourselves imagining their reactions when their stolen loot vanished into thin air. Angela didn't recommend it. First, because the disappearance of stolen riches might just generate more questions. And second, because people with guilty consciences were inclined to retaliate when they thought they had been tricked. Someone who thought they stole precious items from our yard might come back the next day and hold us accountable for their losses.

Besides, we really had to stop people from digging up my yard. Bad enough Loralee was doing it. She couldn't help herself.

~~~~~

Two nights later, Cerb set off the motion sensors. The freaky part was that the lawn decoration gnomes he attacked in my front yard *didn't* set off the sensors. Cerb sensed them coming and went from zero to sixty in about three seconds flat, howling his fury, and leaped through my front window. The video system showed him melting through the glass and landing on a cluster of gnomes that certainly looked like they were marching in formation for my front door. He stomped one, sat on another, caught a third in his jaws and snapped it in half, then turned into a whirlwind and demolished all six in the space of maybe fifteen seconds.

I was still waking up and sliding into my chair, to head to the kitchen and get my phone, when Cerb came into the house. He proudly dropped the debris from his battle on the rug next to my bed. Well, at least I didn't have to sweep up all the pieces. The gnomes didn't bleed blood, but there was something dripping out of them that wasn't dog drool. We bundled up all the pieces in that rug, then into a garbage bag, wrote the rug off as a loss, and prepared for an early morning visit to Divine's.

By that time, Kurt had seen the video feed and came racing over, and we kind of had a good laugh. Not very long. Because the knowledge that Pi Surprise was still trying to get into my house was kind of frightening. Especially when all the beads had been
~~~~~

taken over to Angela's. Couldn't the creeps sense their quarry wasn't at my house any longer?

Actually, that question was a little bit of comfort, because if they couldn't tell the beads had left my place, that meant they wouldn't follow the energy signature of the beads to Angela's. At the same time, the theory was discouraging, because it meant Kerri and her minions would keep trying to get into my house.

What were we going to do?

Maurice suggested that we encourage people to keep trying to dig in my yard, since the gnomes only showed up on nights when we didn't have any treasure hunters. So maybe traffic kept them away.

That led to some seriously ridiculous brainstorming over breakfast. We were all cranky, and maybe the plan we came up with was a little nasty, a little snarky ... but the bozos who kept trespassing on my property were also making me kind of unpopular with my neighbors.

Kurt would increase the alarm system all around my property, including electrifying the fence around the back of the house. We would install an old-fashioned snow fence around the front yard. After getting agreement from the neighbors. Letting them know we were going to punish trespassers would probably put them in a better humor. Several people on adjoining property had complained to me about people trying to get onto my property by going through theirs and climbing the fence. Kurt would also add spotlights on pivots with motion sensors to guide them, to highlight trespassers at night, like the old movies about prison breaks.

When I got to work, I would make some signs. One would go at the end of my driveway, and the others would be hung at strategic points on the fence in the backyard. Basically, I would charge a licensing fee for anyone who wanted to dig in my front yard, on the understanding that they had to put the lawn back the way they found it when they were done digging. That would also serve to short-circuit anyone who would claim they didn't realize they were on private property. Harry actually caught two lame-brains who insisted my lawn was communal property of the neighborhood association, and that gave them the right to dig there. We didn't have a neighborhood association. When Gordon checked their identification, the two were from Michigan and Pennsylvania, not the neighborhood.

At the very least, I would get some money to restore my yard, and maybe improve it. Kurt would get to test out several new security system features he had been working on.

I was in a much better mood when Kurt and I met up outside my old dorm just before open dorms started at noon, to make our first exam of the phone booth. We reminisced about that odd freshman year I spent in the dorm. I had moved back in with my folks after the required on-campus residence year and didn't feel like I was shirking my duty as a guardian. Foiling attempts to break through the dimensional barriers into Neighborlee served to drain away increasingly larger amounts of the enemy's energy. This granted us some time to relax and build up our own strength. I would have wasted my time living on campus. Chances were good that the next attempt wouldn't have been on the WB campus anyway. Every defeated attack on Neighborlee strengthened the barrier in that particular spot.

Of course, if there was something hinky going on with the phone booth, that might just blow our theory of patterns right out of the metaphorical water.

The clock ticked over to noon and it was now legal for outsiders to come into the dorm. Closed floor hours were more relaxed for summer term, so we could both go in and up and Kurt could go onto the girls' side of the floor. Rita was waiting for us. We climbed the stairs in silence. Kurt took over my kinda-sorta flying ability, after I stood up, holding onto the railing at the bottom of the stairs, and managed a hop upward. I always needed something to launch. He flew us up, along with my wheelchair, and we glided up the stairs, with Rita hurrying ahead of us as lookout. It would not be good to run into someone on the stairs and have them see me and Kurt hovering a couple feet above the stair steps, with my wheelchair floating behind us. Granted, it might have been funny, but depending on who saw us, it might leave psychological scars. At the very least, we could have been deafened by terrified, freaked out shrieks.

This would have been much easier if Jane could have helped us, but she had several massages booked at the spa and didn't have anyone to take over for her. If we had to come back, hopefully she would be available to enclose us in the Ghost field, make us invisible, and fly us up to the third floor and through a wall. A lot easier than telekinesis travel.

We got up to my old dorm floor without anyone seeing us. I settled into my wheelchair on the landing and Kurt pushed the door open. No need for a keycard during open dorm hours.

Kurt stopped short, about five steps down the hall. He was leading the way, with Rita behind me, and I almost ran into the back of his calves with my footrests.

"What?" I asked, barely remembering to keep my voice down. We were still close to the stairwell. The door was still open, the pneumatic hinges slowly closing, and my voice would have echoed and attracted the wrong kind of attention.

"It's gone. Something flickered for a few seconds, and then ..." Kurt turned to look back at us. "Okay, it's been a while, but there was something familiar about the energy ripples I saw."

"Familiar how?" I asked. "Big Ugly familiar? Creepy buzzing in the quarries familiar?"

"What about the quarries?" Rita asked. "Something from Black Water followed the kids back here and settled in the phone booth?"

"That's an idea." Kurt thought for a few moments, lips pursed, then he shook his head. "This is kind of ..." He grinned, and I thought maybe he felt a little embarrassed. "It's kind of a photo negative of the energy waves from the time travel watch."

Rita groaned and turned to lean back against the wall. "I knew it. I just knew it. All that stupidity we did when we were living here, it's finally caught up with us."

"Maybe," was all he said, before hitting the ceiling light switch and continuing down the hall.

The phone booth sat right under the ceiling light. At the wrong angle for the reflection that Rita described. I saw a flicker of light, some color, some movement. Weird thing, though. The light I saw wasn't from the ceiling light. For one thing, the ceiling light had a pink film that I swear was the same one someone put up during my freshman year, and the flicker of light and movement in the bottom panel of the phone booth door was blue and green.

"Did you see that?" I asked Kurt, who had flinched but hadn't stopped walking in that moment.

"Yep. The waves came back, just for a second."

"Still think it's the negative of the time travel watch energy or whatever?"

"What does that mean, if it's a negative? It throws you backward in time, instead of forward?" Rita asked. She had gotten over her brief moment of panic and followed us.

We came to a stop against the wall facing the phone booth.

"If you want to get technical," he began.

"Kurt, don't," I said. I could envision him getting into a semi-philosophical lecture on aspects of time travel. He and Rodney sometimes got together and had friendly arguments about bad science in science fiction movies, and that usually led to a few weeks of fun, trying to come up with a working time travel machine or a working model of whatever piece of futuristic technology had triggered the discussion.

"No, please, tell me." Rita offered a smile that certainly looked to me like she was trying not to let her teeth chatter.

"Well, the watch just froze whoever was caught in its field. It didn't really move anyone forward in time. Which is why it's a little freaky that I'm kind of mentally connecting what I saw back then with what I got flickers of here."

Kurt nudged the booth door with just the tips of two fingers. Maybe he was half-expecting to get zapped or scorched from contact, and trying to keep it as minimal as possible.

A whiff of something drifted out to us, there and gone for a second. A chemical smell. Damp. While I was trying to lean closer and get another sniff, to try to identify it, Kurt half-knelt and touched the textured metal floor of the phone booth. We both flinched when a blue-green light flashed, just for a second, on his fingertips. Then they were just damp. He rubbed his fingers together.

"Feels like sand," he muttered.

"Smells like fertilizer," I said, even though that made no sense.

"I swear, I'm going to …" Rita looked a little sick, a little "oh, yeah, right," as she trailed off. Then she offered us a slightly queasy smile. "I knew there was something weird going on with Black Water."

"You want to start from the beginning?" Kurt said.

"Ming, one of the girls in the Black Water science project. Every day like clockwork, she comes in here right after her morning session at the pool, and sits on the phone for an hour with her boyfriend, who's on summer term at Cleveland State. He's some computer nerd who got in trouble and got all his electronics taken away by the judge for six months. She's doing some kind of empathy thing. She won't use her cell phone while he can't use his, so they use their dorm phones. One time I caught her changing out of her bathing suit while she was talking to him. She's constantly getting yelled at by the other girls for leaving puddles in here, or leaving some kind of mess. She has long hair, and it's constantly dripping. It leaves a trail on the dorm floor. The work-study girls complain the most, because they have to mop up all the time, to keep people from falling."

"Sand and fertilizer," I murmured.

"Sand, yeah, I can understand, but not ..." Kurt closed his eyes and nodded. "Yeah, fertilizer. Somehow I knew that night was going to come back to haunt us."

"But it's been over twenty years since those pallets of homemade bombs went in. You'd think it'd be diluted or cycled away or whatever happens in a pond that size. It should have washed away over Pickle Falls by now."

"Are you really dumb enough to expect things to be done the normal way, when it comes to Black Water? This is Neighborlee, remember?"

"Someone want to tell me what you're talking about before I freak?" Rita said.

The door of the bathroom opened. An Asian girl came out, rubbing at her long, wet hair with a towel. She was barefoot, in shorts and T-shirt, and carried a swimsuit over one arm. The other hand held the ubiquitous basket of shower items that I remembered quite well from my year on this dorm floor. She took a couple steps toward the phone booth and then saw us and stopped short. The guilty little grin she gave Rita filled in a few pieces for me. This was Ming, fresh from washing up after diving in Black Water for her life sciences project.

That was a very smart move, getting that water off her, even if delayed. Especially if those pallet loads of fertilizer and other chemicals for making a bomb big enough to destroy Black Water Pool and Pickle Falls were somehow still lingering in the water, strong enough to be smelled. I had a brief mental image of the water eating away at the skin and clothes of those students, if they had too much prolonged contact with it. Maybe it was time to have a talk with the professors in the life sciences department?

Better yet, have Angela have a talk with them. No one, even college professors who thought they knew everything, dared to ignore Angela when she wanted something done, or changed or stopped.

"Sorry," Ming said. "Just figured nobody else was back yet. I could wait to mop up after … you know, after I use the towel and …" She shrugged.

We moved back from the phone booth and she went down on one knee, swiping at the floor and then the seat, which had a puddle on it. The fertilizer aroma faded under the influence of the lemony scent lingering in her towel. It was faint enough I didn't identify it until I saw the bottle of shower gel in her basket. None of us said anything until Ming had finished wiping up after herself and retreated to her dorm room.

"It's all gone," Kurt said. "No more energy." He leaned back against the wall and rubbed his chin and thought. Then he grinned and pulled out his cell phone and headed down the hall as he tapped through the index. "Hey, hon," he said.

That meant he was calling Jane. That one word was about as close as he got to lovey-dovey talk. I had a good idea what he was going to say next.

"Are your appointments done? Think you can take off for a long lunch in the quarries? Lanie and I found something interesting at the dorm, and I think you and I need to team up to do some analyzing." He reached the stairwell and glanced back at me and Rita, as we caught up with him. He winked and grinned. Jane had obviously agreed.

Once I was back down on the ground floor and safely settled in my wheelchair, Kurt hurried off to pick up lunch for him and Jane before they headed out to Black Water. I imagined they would use Jane's Ghost field to go down into the water and investigate without getting wet or needing oxygen tanks. A handy thing, having that particular talent that let Jane fly and go invisible and phase through solid objects. And let Kurt do the same when he borrowed her gift. Rita and I lingered outside for a while before I got in my Jeep and left. She had a right to know some of the background of Black Water Pool and the fertilizer smell. I told her about our first real Senior Prank Night on duty, when we stopped Reggie Grandstone from blowing up Pickle Falls.

"Too bad you had to stop them," Rita said when I finished. She had been in Neighborlee long enough to have had a few bad encounters with the Grandstones. Most of them were the older generation, who weaseled their way into positions they considered prestigious, on various committees and boards for the college. "It would have done the town some good for them to embarrass themselves badly enough to have to leave town. Or just ..." She shrugged. "Well, going through the water treatment plant. Think it really could have happened?"

"I don't want to think about it." I couldn't help grinning as I remembered another detail of those days scrambling to stop the typical arrogant Grandstone idiocy and destruction.

"What? You have to tell me. I need something to laugh about."

"I was just remembering what Felicity said, when we realized they could end up in the water treatment plant. Something along the lines of, 'Water flavored with Grandstone. Ick.' Kind of says it all, you know?"

Rita laughed and agreed.

Chapter Six

That evening, Kurt and Jane came over to report what they had found in Black Water. And what they didn't. No remains of the pallets and the timing equipment that had gone into the water all those years ago. Either someone had dived to retrieve them, or the water had been sufficiently corrosive over the years to devour that metal and wood. Not a comforting thought. Before I could say anything, Kurt said he had already contacted a member of the faculty at WB, to give him the story and advise that students no longer be allowed to dive in the pool. He and Jane took samples of the water from different portions of the pool, and from different depths. They gave some, carefully marked, to that faculty contact to have it analyzed. They took more samples, from every level of Black Water, for Hoax to analyze. Just in case.

Kurt and Jane also found, to our disappointment, that Black Water Pool wasn't bottomless. They found the bottom, with a thick layer of clay-ish sludge, and no plants growing in it. They found no fish or other water creatures within twenty feet of the bottom. They did find plants growing in the sides of the pool and some signs of life at about twenty feet up from the bottom, but nothing below that line. There were some openings in the sides of the pool where water from either springs or the water table under the old quarries fed in. That contributed to and explained the constant flow of water over Pickle Falls.

There were no flashes of light, no ripples of energy, the entire time they were at the pool, no matter how deep they dove. No reaction to the samples of water sitting in sunlight. The water from the deepest portion of the pond, where no life existed, did have a distinct fertilizer odor, but it didn't give off any lights. I was glad when they sealed up the sample jars and packed up everything and left to fly to Hoax. I did not want that stuff in my house.

We updated the rest of the guardians on what we had found and done and learned. Angela provided Rita with an herbal solution of her own devising that would deep clean the phone booth and remove any residue of pond water that might linger. Rita reported that the other girls on the floor were grateful, because they claimed the phone booth stank, a little stronger every day, no matter how well Ming cleaned up after herself. Even when she hung an air deodorizer gel stick from the light in the ceiling of the phone booth.

~~~~~

Maurice was wrong. The jewels and bones taken from the holes in my yard didn't evaporate.

Monday afternoon, the lab investigating the skull contacted Chief Tanner to let him know of a new problem, and he immediately told us. A reconstruction expert had come from a lab in Columbus to work on the skull, to try to get an idea of what the dead person had looked like when alive. They pulled the skull out of the locked cabinet and it was visibly different from what they had put into the cabinet the week before. A few tests revealed the skull was chalk, not bone. The lab people couldn't claim that they had been duped, because samples taken from the skull when it was originally turned over to them, to try to find DNA for testing, had proven it was bone. The hip bones found elsewhere in my yard were immediately tested. They were still bone.

Chief Tanner followed up on a hunch, which was always a wise thing to do when dealing with Neighborlee weirdness. He asked for an examination, discretely handled, of the jewels found in my yard. The gem experts dealing with them were reluctant to do so. A jeweler from Ontario had obtained a court order to prohibit anything being done with the pearls and emeralds. They weren't to be examined or analyzed until he arrived. He believed they were part of a collection stolen from him six years ago. The Chief was a very persuasive guy and convinced the gem experts they needed more documentation than had been done already. Especially if someone else showed up claiming the jewels belonged to them.

When the vault was opened, the pearls and emeralds were visibly plastic gems, very low quality, with the seams from the molds visible. They were now suitable only for little girl dress-up games. However, the rubies and sapphires were examined and found to still be genuine.

I had to wonder how long that would last.

When the Ontario jeweler was contacted, he responded with a
~~~~~

second lawsuit, accusing the gemologists of stealing his property to sell, and took an earlier flight than planned. When he arrived on Tuesday, Chief Tanner and his team were ready. They had documentation and security footage to prove no one had opened the vault until the check on the state of the jewels on Monday. The vault had been sealed with tape and official stamps, and remained locked until he showed up.

This time when they opened the vault and the sealed boxes, the pearls and emeralds were gone. A check of the box holding the rubies and sapphires now revealed plastic bits that didn't even look like an attempt to be counterfeit or costume gems. They looked like the plastic shavings from craft kits, to create pictures and then melt with an iron.

The same security had been applied to the bones. When the forensics experts opened up the containers, on video record, the chalk skull had also vanished from its locked compartment in the lab. The hip bones had changed from bone to thick cardboard.

So, the next time Loralee dug in my backyard, we just filled in the hole and tried not to see what she had temporarily dug up from another dimension. It wasn't worth the trouble.

This whole warped allergic reaction and its impact on her pregnancy was starting to get on my nerves, and my brothers'. It was also trying the patience and friendliness of our neighbors. They had to deal with people from out of town and various thick-headed representatives of the media. The ones who were stupid enough to insist that the notion of privacy was outdated. They self-righteously insisted the world, starting with their network or news syndicate, had a right to know what was going on under *my lawn*. They acted insulted and claimed their rights were being violated every time we said no to interviews. Felicity helped out when she could, killing cameras and voice recorders and any other electrical equipment they carried, with a well-aimed EM burst. For a while, those media invaders accused us of damaging their expensive equipment, but they couldn't prove we had an invisible electrical fence around the house.

That snow fence we put up just reinforced the certainty among the treasure hunters and general idiots that we did indeed have something to hide. We made the sign demanding a digging fee even bigger, and Pete painted it in luminescent paint, so it glowed in the dark. The invasion didn't really last that long, according to the calendar, but it seemed to go on for years.

"Could you ask if she has any idea when the babies are due?" I asked Maurice when he was over the house, visiting one evening. I didn't want to ask, because I really did like having Loralee and Cerb around. There were just some things that couldn't go on as they were for much longer. Life was complicated enough in Neighborlee without bringing in outsiders who seemed impervious to the general, defensive atmosphere of "Go away, we don't like you, we don't want you here."

He asked. Loralee gave a mournful little moan, shuddered, and tried to dig down deeper in the nest of blankets. Other than waddling trips out into the yard to do her business, and when she sleep-dug in the backyard, she wasn't moving from the bedroom anymore.

"Sorry. She says she's really sorry, but she doesn't know. She's the first one to get pregnant while on duty here on Earth, in an alternate form. Kind of makes things difficult to figure out," Maurice added with a shrug. It did weird things to the fluttering of his wings. He kind of bobbed sideways in the air, hovering there at eye level with me.

~~~~~

We couldn't identify who, but we had our suspicions that some friends in high places felt sorry for our struggles, and they stepped in to do what they could. Word leaked and spread, a little too slow for our taste, but at least it did. Finally, the right people heard about the jewels and bones turning into cheap plastic reproductions. No reaction for a few days, until our friendly leak added pictures and documentation, to prove it. That finally killed the enthusiasm of the treasure hunters. But not before we had a few more encounters with people trying to climb over the fence or pull into the driveway and start digging without paying the fee. People weren't invading our parents' property, though, because we regularly applied the smelliest possible deer repellant on the market, every other night. That worked better than a snow fence.

That might have been wasted effort. The renters kept the outdoor security floodlights on all night, and stepped outside with a rifle every time they thought they heard movement outside, or a car slowed down and seemed about to pull into the driveway. The
~~~~~

rifle was a toy, but the treasure hunters didn't know that. Funny, but nobody who got threatened with that toy rifle ever complained to the police.

The trespassers kept insisting they didn't see the signs demanding they pay to dig. Then they got angry or acted all injured innocence, when Harry or I told them they had to pay the fee for digging even though they didn't find anything before we caught them. They got even angrier when we told them it was $100 per hour, flat rate, no prorating for short duration of the dig.

Hey, they didn't ask what the fee was before they started digging. Any lawyer would agree that they had agreed to our terms the moment they stepped onto the grass and took that first shovelful. I even consulted with Mr. Carr, of Carr, Cooper and Crenshaw, and he agreed with me. It was on the sign, making it all legitimate. If they were in too much of a hurry to read all the conditions posted on the sign, that was their problem, not ours. Being in a hurry to dig and trying to do it really quietly to avoid being caught kind of proved they knew they were in the wrong.

Word got around about how we were stiffing "honest" treasure hunters. That, combined with the news of the plastic gems, finally gave us peace by the start of July.

Even better, the treasure hunters and the stink of the deer repellant irritated the troublesome renters at our folks' farmhouse. They decided they wanted out. They packed up and left over Fourth of July weekend, and didn't ask for their security deposit back.

We decided we had had enough dealing with renters. Pete and Harry got to work on heavy duty cleaning and fixing up things that the renters hadn't taken care of, per our rental agreement. We agreed to lock up the house tight and secure until Mum and Pop came home. Maybe the boys would move out to the farmhouse and live there, to provide security. I was just so glad to get those people out of my parents' home without a legal battle, I decided not to track them down and slap them with the rental agreement and all the terms they had violated. It just wasn't worth it.

Besides, having the farmhouse empty of strangers kind of gave us a sense of hope. Maybe someday soon, we would get word about our parents and they would be coming home.

~~~~~
~~~~~

Kurt called me, mid-morning the next weekend, while the boys and I were inspecting the house and making a list of all the things we needed to do to make it ready for Mum and Pop. He asked me if I had had any dreams.

"Blue dreams?" I asked, and shivered a little.

Because I hadn't dreamed one in several weeks, much to ours and Stanzers' disappointment. Yet this morning I kept looking around, looking out the nearest window, expecting to see storm clouds. I kept hearing a rumbling of thunder, loud and sharp and yet with a distinct sensation that it was far away.

"I don't know," he finally said after a long pause, just short of getting me nervous enough to shout and ask if he was still there. "I've just got all this buzzing in the air, coming through the ground. It didn't last long. I was hoping maybe you had a warning."

I hadn't. I promised I would try to pay attention if I dreamed that night. Yeah, and how could I suddenly put controls on my dreams, when I hadn't managed that yet?

It turned out I didn't need to. Mid-afternoon, London contacted me via email and asked me to go over to Stanzer's office. She was going to send him something she had found, and she was sure he would need a friend there when he read it.

Stanzer was checking the Weather Channel when I arrived, his fingers tangling as he slammed his keyboard, drawing up pictures from multiple satellites and weather watcher groups and news stations all around Ohio, Michigan, Indiana, Pennsylvania, and into Canada. So many of them had pictures of lightning. Blue-tinged lightning. After about ten minutes of going through the images with him, I picked up a pattern. It was always the same single lightning bolt. Only one had been tinged blue. We went through the images from the storm, from multiple sources, and still, only that one bolt of lightning.

The storm, according to all the official and unofficial sources, had lasted less than five minutes. It struck an open area, farmland, far west of us, an area less than two miles in radius, straddling the Turnpike as it headed for Sandusky.

The storm had struck early in the morning, arrived with no warning and then vanished with no damage to the surrounding countryside. As far as anyone knew. One news helicopter had a glimpse of activity on the Turnpike, cars on the side of the northbound lane and others sitting in ditches. When Stanzer tried to access the image for a closer look, he got a message that it had just been removed.

"Huh," he said, and narrowed his eyes at the message on the screen as if he could read something else in the words.

For a second I had an awful suspicion he was going to ask a Hound to show up and somehow do something to the computer, infiltrate the Internet, to get the information he wanted.

"Umm, London said she was sending you something you needed to see," I said.

Stanzer frowned and clicked on his email, bringing it up on the screen. No new message. My phone buzzed in my pocket and I pulled it out to find a text. London was sending it now.

"She wanted me to be here with you when you got it," I explained. I felt like I was the one who needed an explanation about now.

His email chimed and a new message popped into the queue. It had a number of attachments, and opened up before Stanzer could move the mouse to click on it.

London was obviously in charge of the playback, choosing the information and the order in which Stanzer viewed it.

First came police dispatcher reports, several from people in the southbound Turnpike lane, reporting seeing a van chasing a pickup truck, and shots fired. There were no images. The people heading south passed the conflict in the northbound lanes before they realized what was going on. I was kind of relieved, even though there wasn't much to go on yet. After all, if something had happened that affected a member of the Hunt, to bring that one strike of blue lightning, then chances were good someone Stanzer knew had been in the pickup being chased by the van. And was being shot at.

Next, London played audio of conversations between FBI agents. They were searching for an agent who had infiltrated an organization headed by someone named Archby. London inserted an abbreviated dossier on a crime syndicate boss, Archby, with a record nasty enough and long enough to make me grateful when London closed it down again. Stanzer looked pale, and pressed his mouth flat until his lips were nearly white.

The missing agent was to meet his contacts with important

information he had taken from Archby's headquarters. He had car trouble, he had been shot, his phone was running out of power, and he knew Archby's men were following him.

The next report was the result of following the onboard GPS to find the agent's car at a Turnpike rest stop, pushed around back behind the building so it was out of sight. The engine was still warm, so he hadn't been away from it long. There were three cars of agents involved in the search. A dark van suspected of being Archby's had pulled out of the rest stop just as the three cars of agents were pulling in. Two cars headed out immediately, once they determined the missing agent was not in his car. The third car of agents stayed to begin searching, in hopes of some clue to where he hid that vital information.

The next report was of the freak storm, visible on the highway ahead of the two cars of agents.

A long slide show of images followed, interspersed with bits and pieces of FBI reports. The investigation was ongoing, because the authorities were dealing with what looked like a collision of the van and truck mentioned in the dispatch calls. They were also busy fending off local emergency services, the highway patrol, and local authorities.

An old pickup truck lay on its side, halfway into the ditch on the right side of the road. Scorch marks streaked the highway. Smoke rose up in the air from where bushes and weeds along the roadside had been burning. The van lay on the other side of the road, on its top, smoking, with long streaks that looked like the paint had been melted off it.

There were eight bodies. London showed them in the order in which they had been found, with the preliminary reports. Four were young people, two male and two female, age estimates between late teens and early twenties. All had road rash, bruises, cuts, and lay scattered along the road where they had been thrown from the truck when it had been forced off the road at high speed and had flipped. All had been shot and killed at close range, with multiple gunshots. They had been searched, their possessions taken. Debris along the side of the road, what hadn't been touched by the flames, included tickets for Cedar Point, the amusement park in Sandusky, and a printout of directions to get to the park. The entire printout wasn't there, or hadn't been found yet. Maybe it had been burned in the multiple small fires surrounding the truck. Without that initial first page, there was no indication where the group heading up to the lake had originated. No identification. The truck had been damaged by the fire as well and the vin plate and other paperwork had either burned or been taken when the victims were searched.

Three of the dead bodies were men already identified as being in the employ of Archby. They all showed massive burns across their bodies, with holes burned in their clothes and hair scorched away. The coroner on the scene couldn't say for sure yet, but made a preliminary guess of electrocution. For all she knew, they had been hit by the lightning from the freak storm. Agents on site were guessing the van had been hit by a lightning bolt, which explained it being tossed across the Turnpike lanes and burning the paint in places.

The eighth body was the missing agent. He also had been thrown from the truck. Preliminary examination indicated he had died of blood loss. Some attempt had been made to tend his injuries, meaning he had been shot before the collision and attack. The agents on site guessed the young people in the truck had stopped to help him. The information stolen from Archby's headquarters wasn't on him.

There was one survivor. A girl, mid-teens, dark hair, injuries consistent with being thrown from the truck, but no gunshot wounds. No signs of electrocution. No burns. She was comatose. Preliminary examination as she was loaded into the ambulance listed several birthmarks and made special note of the rings of thin scars on both wrists.

The girl was considered a key witness and the only lead to where the information the agent had died to obtain might be hidden. The agent in charge had taken her into custody and she was being moved to a secure facility to be tended.

An addendum filed just a few minutes before London asked me to go to Stanzer said the girl's brain was emitting electrical activity the doctors had never seen before, very low level. There was no way to predict when she would wake from her coma, or if she ever would.

"Where did they take her?" Stanzer asked.

"I'm sorry," London said, her voice coming through his

computer. A moment later, the images shut down and her face appeared on the screen. "I've sent you everything Sherwood and I have been able to dig up so far. We're searching out the agent in charge and his team, to try to locate them."

"Maybe safe houses in the area?" I suggested. Yeah, bad influence from TV thrillers and spy dramas, which all the experts say have very little resemblance to real life FBI and intelligence agency or police practices. "If she's sick, maybe they don't dare move her? Go to ground right away?"

"Good idea," Stanzer said with a nod, still staring at the screen, as if he could see the reports that weren't there anymore. He took a deep breath, loud, as if he hadn't been breathing the whole time we read through the reports and studied the images. "Thank you."

"I'm sorry," London said again. "It's not the kind of news I wanted to give you --"

"No, it's okay. At least it's something. Can you get me any closer and clearer images of the girl? Maybe clean her up, get rid of the bruising and the blood?"

"It's been fourteen years since you arrived here on Earth," I said. "She would have been what, three or four years old at the most? Would she remember anything?"

"That lightning was from a Hound intervening, protecting her," Stanzer said, finally turning away from the computer. "They will react to pain and fear, but they are our guardians, our partners, and the older we get, the less they act without our asking, or at least communicating that we need help. For a Hound to be there, protecting her, she would have to be in contact with it. Somehow."

"Then why didn't the Hound do something as soon as they realized they were being chased, or when the shooting started?" I had to ask.

Stanzer stared at me a moment, then shrugged. I really hated driving that flicker of light, of hope from his eyes. It had only been there for a few seconds.

"For a long time, I lost ... not hope, but I didn't believe as strongly as I should have. Other than my scars, I really didn't have much in the way of proof that I was from another world." He snorted. "My scars and a pocket full of gems. As a firstborn, one of the older children, I was entrusted with gems and gold to help pay for whatever we needed to survive in whatever alien world the

Hounds brought us. We really didn't expect to be separated, and to have it so hard to find each other. Fortunately, I was found by good people, and the foster care system that took me in was ethical, and I didn't lose any of that wealth. It paid for my education, financed my search, paid for this building, to prepare to house us when I find others of the Hunt. I just don't understand why it took so long."

"Do you remember many of the others?" I asked. I wasn't sure if I should keep him talking, if it would hurt. Maybe he needed to talk through the pain. How many people could he talk to about his friends, his home, all the years he had been searching and preparing and feeling so alone?

What would life be like for Stanzer if he hadn't found Neighborlee, and found people he could talk to about the otherness in his life? People who would understand and be there for him, without recommending he get serious medication and serious therapy.

I could guess, because I had considered what my life would be like if I hadn't been dropped into Neighborlee when I was a toddler.

"All of them. I've made lists over the years, I've tried to recreate our family crests, maps of our clan holdings, the Aerie ..." Stanzer went utterly still, and I was sure he had stopped breathing again.

"What?" I seriously considered slapping him to get his brain or at least his lungs working again.

"The Aerie. I saw the resemblance years ago, but I just didn't ... what if it's a clue?" He got up so fast he nearly toppled forward, which would have sent him sprawling across me and my chair.

Stanzer caught himself and twisted sideways just in time. He darted out of his office, into the back room. I heard the squeak of a file drawer opening. He came out, holding a large piece of folded paper in one hand and a faded gold cloth-covered journal. He unfolded the paper, and his hands were shaking. His grin was crooked as he spread it out on the second desk on the other side of the office, which seemed to be used for sorting things. Right now, his PI business was a one-man operation. Maybe he was waiting for more members of the Hunt to show up, to make them his business partners?

"What does that look like?" he said, then coughed a chuckle and gave the paper a half-turn.

"Lake Erie?" I guessed. Except the blue surrounded the outline, instead of being inside the outline. The islands -- South Bass, Kelly's Island, North Bass, the other little ones -- were all filled in blue.

"Exactly. But that's not the lake. That's the Aerie. It's an island, and I'm not really sure what the name was long ago, but ... it's a meeting place for the clan heads, the Firstborn of the Firstborn, the strongest of the gifted. It's where our parents met to conduct business, to arrange marriages ..." He closed his eyes a moment and took a deep breath, and I saw pain ripple across his face.

"Stanzer? Are you okay? Maybe you should sit down."

"No, I'm okay." He took a deep breath. "We keep the gifts within our families. The firstborn is always the strongest, the secondborn is the support, the backup. The thirdborn is always the firstborn child of the secondborn of the previous generation. I was firstborn of Clan Seras. My sister, Lin, was secondborn. Our cousin, Jilliam, firstborn of our uncle, our father's younger brother, was thirdborn." Another deep breath. "Dandova was thirdborn for Clan Kale. Marriages are always arranged between firstborn and thirdborn, for alliances and to keep the talents, the strengths and gifts in the ruling families. We were good friends even before our families betrothed us."

"How old is she now?"

"She's four years younger than me, so she's twenty-four."

"Oh. Okay." I understood now. The girl we saw in those few pictures, covered with blood and bruises, so pale, the only one from the accident not entirely covered with a white sheet, was in her teens. Too young to be Dandova. Too young for Stanzer's hope.

"There are four girls she could be," Stanzer said after a few moments of us just looking at each other. He picked up the journal where he had dropped it on his desk and opened it up.

Chapter Seven

For the next hour, I just sat and listened and let him talk. Going through the lists he had made over the years. Looking at the maps he had made from memories. Hearing stories of adventures, exploring or traveling with his father and uncle to learn their territory and start training for his duties as the head of the clan. He had drawn images of the clan symbols, drew diagrams of the buildings he had been in when he visited other clans. Stanzer was a good artist, visibly improving as he made multiple drawings of the same people over the years. I estimated he had bought the journal when he was maybe in middle school, to help him remember, to organize the pieces of memories in his head so they wouldn't be lost or warped or faded.

He had three pages of sketches of Dandova, as a little girl, then the ten-year-old he had seen last, then several sketches of attempts to guess what she would look like now.

"I don't suppose it would do any good to put those into whatever search engine the AI's are using to help with looking for the Hunt? Maybe get hold of some of that software that takes a picture and morphs it into what someone looked like ten years ago, and then ten years in the future?"

Stanzer just shook his head a few times, then he slumped back in his chair and closed his eyes and laughed. Softly. A little ragged. Showing just how tired this whole effort made him, in his spirit if not his body.

"Never .... Well, it isn't that I never thought of it, because I did once or twice, but ... I can't really be sure how close these drawings are to the real people. And honestly, I'm afraid to put that much information out there."

"Like if this guy hunting all of you managed to follow you to Earth, and he gets some kind of alert and uses the drawings to track you down?" I guessed.

"Something like that. When our parents were trying to find some way of protecting us, disquieting rumors were coming to light. Some clan heads were dealing with Gahlmorag on their own, making deals, trying to get special treatment. Essentially betraying the alliance, betraying our vows to Hamin to protect the people entrusted to our care. If their parents were traitors, there is always a chance they also vowed falsely to Hamin and the Hunt. If they came to Earth, they could be hunting us, to turn us over to Gahlmorag if he ever follows us to Earth."

"That kind of sucks."

That earned another weary chuckle from him.

"That is the result of many long, dark hours of fearing the worst, imagining the worst. What could be worse than finding out I'm the only one who made it to Earth, that all the others were caught before their parents could send them into the void in the Hounds' care? What if they landed here on Earth and they were caught by traitors? What if the people who found them didn't show them any sympathy or mercy, and those who told the truth of what we were ... were considered insane, or dangerous?"

"Yeah, Earth doesn't have a really good track record of dealing with aliens from other worlds. We expect them to be ready to suck our brains and eat us for lunch. Or rip away all our resources and leave Earth an empty rock. Or they treat the friendly aliens like menaces and get into further trouble and waste all the good chances offered them."

"Them?" Stanzer raised one eyebrow in question, and maybe teasing me a little.

"Hey, I could possibly be an illegal alien just as much as you."

"True." He shrugged and that weary smile wiped away some of the aching that glowed like dying embers in his eyes.

"Hey, London, are you still listening?"

"I am almost done with the rendering of the survivor," London responded.

Heck if she didn't sound a little distracted, like she wasn't able to handle several thousand calculations or functions or whatever, all in a split second. Maybe we really were being a bad influence on her, and Sherwood, and they were becoming more like real Humans all the time.

"That's great," I said. "What are the chances of tracking down some kind of uber-secret government operation that managed to snatch up a bunch of kids who all arrived in freak storms, like the one this morning? Maybe locked them away in a place like Area 51, or maybe the underground lair of the Rivals?"

"Col. Hayward asked me to specifically search all the data confiscated from the Rivals' records depot, to determine if there were any other locations like the one that destroyed itself with the genetically engineered disease. No matches have appeared yet, so chances are very good, and increasing every day as we clear and verify more data, that the Rivals never even learned about the Hunt, much less found and imprisoned them."

"That's not exactly what Lanie was asking," Stanzer said. "But thank you, that's comforting."

"The meteorological data from this morning's storm is helping us narrow down the factors necessary to identify where other members of the Hunt might have arrived on Earth. However, the technology adequate to detect the energy levels and capture images and harvest other data from the storm did not exist fourteen years ago. This makes searching the records harder. Vital data is missing, because it never registered to begin with."

"Plus all the records of children gone missing or found wandering with no identification, that's a lot to sort through," I offered. I had experience with searching for and searching through data relating to missing or unidentified children, back when most records were only on paper.

"I'm so stupid." He snapped his fingers and snatched up the map of the Aerie he had been showing me. "This is why I brought it out in the first place. Hearing those kids were driving up to Cedar Point triggered … Okay, the shape of Lake Erie is so much like the outline of the island that supported the Aerie, and we all had clan houses on its shores. I had the craziest idea that the coincidence of the shape of the island and the lake could be a clue of some kind, and that's what brought me to Ohio in the first place. Neighborlee, this general area, sort of matches up with my clan's territory, back home."

"So you think maybe the other kids came through to places surrounding Lake Erie?" I played with the idea after I had said it aloud. "London, what do you think? Does that help you narrow down where you need to search?"

"I will need more data on your home territory, Stanzer," she said after a pause of a few seconds. "All the maps, all the drawings you gave me. Perhaps the other members of the Hunt have also recorded the emblems and drawn from their memories, and they are using them, like a flag to get the attention of the rest of the Hunt."

When I left Stanzer's office, he was busy scanning each page of that battered journal and uploading it to London. He didn't look tired anymore.

~~~~~

Loralee had one more massive digging campaign in my back yard. In the space of one night, she went out through the wall of the laundry room six times. She dug a hole for maybe three minutes each time, and each time returned to her nest in the bedroom, never waking up. None of those holes had anything in them, according to the video cameras on tiny drones Kurt created just for that purpose. He had programmed them to fly out and take pictures in infrared and night vision and ordinary flash bulb camera, each time Loralee's activities tripped the motion sensors.

The seventh time she went out, there was one last, stubborn treasure hunter spying over the back fence. We found night vision goggles in his backpack when he ran away, screaming in terror.

Why did he scream in terror?

Let's just say that only a fool comes between a pregnant interdimensional visitor trapped in the shape of a dog and the hole she was still in the process of digging.

The video record showed him vaulting over the fence almost the moment Loralee turned away from the hole to go back into the house. He went straight for the hole. The drone swooped in to take pictures, and this idiot swatted it away. Stupid move. He swatted it straight at Loralee. Even more stupid move.

He didn't run when the drone hit her and she turned around and snarled. Doubly stupid move. Especially when that snarl echoed off the surrounding houses in a way that didn't make sense, without a synthesizer and amplifiers giving it reverb. The echo woke up everybody else in the house. Loralee leaped the ten feet back to the hole in one jump, teeth bared and shooting off angry orange sparks from her fur. Kind of like Felicity used to do when she didn't have control of her EM pulses.

The idiot treasure hunter very stupidly stood there and shouted for her to get away, it was his and she couldn't have it.

What was his? There was nothing visible in the hole.
~~~~~

Maybe the guy was delusional?

Pete came tearing out of the house with his light saber. The guy shrieked and ran for the fence, proving that crooks are indeed stupid, gullible people. Or else that shade of green was far more threatening than any of us realized. He slipped when he tried to vault over, and fell, catching his waist on the inverted Vs at the top of the fence. Harry came out of his apartment with his Nerf cannon.

My brothers were brave, kind of dumb, and such geeks. My heroes.

Cerb burst through the wall, glowing with lightning bolts swirling all around him, and went for the guy, who was trying to wriggle free of the fence. His mistake was kicking when Loralee got hold of his sneaker with her jaws. What's worse than coming between a pregnant dog and the hole she just dug? Kicking that pregnant dog when her mate is aimed right at you.

Cerb hit the guy and knocked him free. He fell head-first into the next neighbor's back yard, which happened to be a muddy swamp because he had been emptying his above-ground pool into the swale between our yards. He couldn't control the algae problem and was starting over. First he had to get rid of the noxious pea soup he had been brewing. What the treasure hunter fell into, with his mouth open, shrieking in terror … it wasn't pretty. Can't say he didn't deserve it.

He left shreds of his black T-shirt and his jeans and some skin on the jagged teeth of the fence.

Surfaced from the greeny-muddy swamp. Still shrieking.

Scrambled to his feet, and ran.

Cerb didn't go after him. He wrapped himself around Loralee, crooning and whimpering enough to bring tears to my eyes, even though I knew she was all right.

We were glad we had all the video records of that night's weird invasion, just in case the guy came back and sued us for his injuries, or maybe for sending dangerous beasts after him. We told Gordon, and he helped us write up the report so it didn't sound too crazy, and gave it to Chief Tanner. And then we settled back to wait.

Nothing from the intruder. No lawsuits.

Even better, Loralee stopped digging after that night. We had to wonder if waking her up the first time she went sleep-digging would have solved the problem.

~~~~~

Col. Hayward came back to town with some slightly disturbing news. It turned out the rumors all these years about the pond that resulted from Jinx Longfellow's senior prank were partially true. His team had been trying to create a light show, on what they thought was dry ground. A small explosion in the hole where the team planted the light show broke through a shelf of rock and accessed a spring. The combination of chemicals did create the light effects Jinx and his friends had gone for, but in the water, not just sitting on the ground. The "men in black" who came to check the pond every year were EPA personnel. The light show had died out after two days as planned, but they had some genuine concerns. Something in the water was digging the hole of the pond a little deeper every year. The EPA people wanted to ensure the chemical reaction didn't penetrate to affect the water table in the surrounding area.

After all these years, something odd was happening in the water of the small pond. Odd for Neighborlee, or odd for most other parks and surrounding towns? That was the question. When the government agents came to take their yearly samples this summer, they found traces of fertilizer in the water now. Analysis identified the fertilizer as a chemical balance that hadn't been manufactured in twenty-some years. Hayward decided that couldn't be a coincidence. Not after we had reported to him what Kurt and Jane had found out about Black Water Pool. Maybe what the environmental people had feared all these years had finally happened -- there was penetration from one freaky body of water to another. Either Black Water Pool had eroded through the rock to infiltrate the water table that fed Jinx's pond, or the pond water had touched the water table feeding Black Water. They were maybe half a mile distant.

Kurt and Jane flew to the pond and got samples. They used the Ghost field to travel through the rock, and couldn't find any kind of passageway, not even something as small as half an inch wide, that would channel water from the pool to the pond, or the other direction. They did the same with Black Water. There was no visible connection. So how did the fertilizer suddenly appear in the water of the pond?

On a hunch, we checked with Rita, and found out she had been
~~~~~

sick for the last week, laid up with a stupid summer cold. The first summer term had ended, and most of the girls on third and second floor of Wickslow Hall had gone home, including Ming. She logically thought the problem of water in the phone booth had ended.

So we were a little disturbed to go to the third floor and find a puddle of water two inches deep sitting in the bottom of the phone booth.

That water didn't move, but it had ripples of light moving across it.

Rita, Hayward, Kurt, Jane and I were all there, in the quiet hallway. Not much had changed since the last time I was on the floor. There were a few posters on the bulletin board across from the bathroom door. I found it kind of funny that the floor supervisor wasn't on top of things like Mercedes had been when I was a freshman here. There were announcements for activities all through the school year, which hadn't been removed as they expired. Posters asking for people to help with the community Halloween party. Posters and a sign-up sheet for snacks for the dorm Christmas party. Reminders for the girls to check up on their "secret sis" and encourage them with a card, a candy bar, a note.

There was a plastic sword hanging from the frame of the bulletin board, and a faded sticky note asking who had lost part of their Halloween costume. Either nobody in the dorm had lost it, or they were embarrassed to admit it. The sword was one of those cheapy, hollow blades that no swashbuckler would be caught dead with. Especially since really cool, realistic swords could be borrowed from the theater department. Seeing the sword, though, reminded me of my first Halloween with my folks. Mum dressed up as Zorro and had this really cool sword. It was real.

All but two doors were open on the floor, showing empty dorm rooms. Those doors were at the end of the hall closest to the stairwell. Both those girls were out the whole day doing their summer internship program with local churches, helping run Vacation Bible School. Rita checked with them later, to ask if they had noticed the water in the phone booth. They never noticed because they never used the phone booth. The only one who had ever used the phone booth was Ming. There was no telling how long the phone booth door had been closed.

We opened the door, saw the light ripples, and then the smell swirled through the hallway.

It was sort of a fall smell, rather than muddy, green, with a hint of fertilizer, but not the same chemical fertilizer smell from the last time we had been on the floor. The smell reminded me of the last lawn mowing of the year, on a crisp night with the smell of candles. And I said so, without really meaning to speak aloud.

"And cider and pumpkins," Hayward said, with a hint of a chuckle in his voice. "Which doesn't make any sense." He shrugged and smiled at me. "Reminds me of the first time we met. I don't know why."

"Uh, does anybody else see that?" Jane pointed at the phone booth door.

I rolled my chair back to get at the right angle, since the door was folded open. A shiver ran down from my scalp to my toes, as I watched a scene playing out in the glass panel of the door. It was freakishly familiar.

Kids were walking down a street, dressed in Halloween costumes. A woman in a Zorro costume walked with a little girl in a woods faerie outfit -- me.

"Hey," Kurt began.

The image wavered and died a moment later.

"So what just happened?" Rita gave us a lopsided smile. "I'm kind of glad you guys seemed to see that too. I would be worried that I was hallucinating. Unless I'm hallucinating all of you being here?"

"She fits in far too well with all of you," Hayward grumbled. He leaned back against the wall and crossed his arms and stared at the glass panel in the door of the phone booth, as if willing it to show him the scene again, or maybe show him something different.

"So ... do we wipe up all that water, send it away for testing?" Kurt said. "Or do we leave it here and experiment?"

"Experiment how?" Jane said.

"Maybe the view is different inside the phone booth."

"How did the water get there, if the kids who were studying Black Water aren't here anymore?" I had to ask.

It wasn't like we could interrogate the pool and get coherent answers.

Jane and Kurt ended up doing the experiment. The Ghost field let them get into the dormitory late at night, while the only two residents were asleep, or during the day when they were gone and dorms were closed to outsiders. They floated up to the third floor, outside the wall where the phone booth sat, and phased in through the wall just enough to see what was going on inside the booth. The Ghost field kept them out of phase, and they never touched the water. No telling what effect that water might have on anyone who touched it. They were studying the effect on the phone booth, not living people, after all.

Four days in a row, late at night and mid-morning, they turned themselves invisible and flew over to the campus and hovered halfway in and halfway out of the phone booth, waiting for a light show. No light show, much less visions like that first Halloween after Mum and Pop adopted me, when Col. Hayward met up with us while we were trick-or-treating.

Discussing that one vision we all shared actually gave us our first clue, and some idea of controlling the images.

It turned out that Kurt was thinking about that Halloween, too. There were three of us there that afternoon, all thinking about the same moment in time. So maybe there had to be people present, focused on something, to trigger -- what? A window into a different time?

We were still coming up with that theory, the long way around, when Stanzer got his breakthrough. London had tracked down the identity of the agent in charge of the task force focused on the crime syndicate run by Archby. She located a small nursing home that had gone out of business and had been sitting empty for more than ten years now, since a larger, more modern facility had been built in a more accessible area five miles down the road. There appeared to be water and gas turned on for that building for the first time in those ten years. Electricity had been on all along, to keep the fire alarm and security systems functioning. Satellite surveillance detected activity around the building. Not much, but there were men walking patrols on the flat roofs and in the woods surrounding it, and radio and phone activity inside the building, tracked through GPS.

Stanzer went to investigate. We went to Pastor Rocky, to put him on the special, unspoken prayer list, for the real prayer warriors to deal with.

London confided in me that she was worried about Stanzer. The girl who had been found in the accident matched one of the aged progression images she had created, based on pictures Stanzer had uploaded into her system. There were only two girls in the Hunt young enough to be around fifteen or sixteen, the estimated age of the injured girl, yet Stanzer's drawings of their older brothers or sisters or cousins didn't provide any family resemblance to the girl from the accident scene photos. She looked like the aged progression images of Dandova Kale, Stanzer's betrothed. But Dandova was twenty-four, not sixteen. There was something wrong, something off here. All we could do was pray that Stanzer would find the answers, and be ready to race to help him, if he called us. We had made him promise he would call us if he ran into trouble, if he needed any kind of backup or support.

The night after Stanzer left, I joined Kurt and Jane to visit the dorm and test our new theory. We hovered there, partially inside the dorm and phone booth, for nearly two hours, focusing on shared memories. Not a single flicker of light in one panel of the phone booth door, much less a discernible image. We even tried thinking about that night when Hayward had been taking Toby and Steve to safety and the Rivals nearly captured them. I had been there, spying on Jane and her friend in my dreams, when they raced to the rescue. That had to be a pretty intense, emotional time. Maybe emotions would help?

When I suggested that, Kurt cautiously discounted it, because Trick-or-Treat wasn't really emotional for us. It was fun. I was curious about this stranger in a uniform who showed up to talk to my folks. He was probably curious about me, but there was nothing strongly emotional to trigger a broadcast of what we had shared.

Maybe Kurt was right, or maybe his skepticism cast doubt and drained the energy away. Jane and I focused on our memories of that night of the attempted kidnapping, what I had seen and she had done, until we were repeating ourselves and quite frankly getting a little headachy.

It wasn't that late at night, and we knew Angela was interested in our experiment. We flew over to Divine's and found Angela and Maurice outside, sitting on her swing, looking down over the park. There were a dozen or so candles circling them, and it struck me as a little funny to catch the scent of citronella. It was such an ordinary, normal thing. Why would Angela need citronella to protect her from bugs?

We landed, Jane turned off the Ghost field, and Kurt helped me walk over to sit down on the swing with Angela. She offered us wands and pipes, and we spent a few minutes blowing bubbles. We created thousands of bubbles that all shimmered in the darkness, catching the starlight and moonlight and candlelight. It was kind of relaxing. Telling her about our disappointing evening came easily and didn't take much time.

"What exactly are you guys trying to do?" Maurice said.

The three of us were silent for a few seconds. Then Jane grinned and flopped back on the grass where she had been sitting next to Kurt, and laughed. He was next. I was trying to decide whether to feel like an idiot or get irritated with them, or laugh too.

"I guess we got so caught up in figuring out how to trigger more visions, we kind of lost track of our goal," I said after a few seconds. For punctuation, I blew hard on the neon green meerschaum pipe and blew a waterfall of bubbles that smelled slightly of spearmint.

"That's because we really didn't have one, did we?" Jane said.

"Well, it's kind of understood," Kurt said, stretching out next to her, "we need to figure out what's going on, and then we can figure out if we need to shut it down or not."

"True," Angela said. "But wouldn't a good first step be figuring out how it's happening? It sounds like the water is involved. Maybe if you stop the water from coming, you don't have to worry about how it works, because you stop it right there. Time travel is a tricky thing."

"Can't do it," Maurice said. "Every kind of law of physics and space and time has one rule they all share. Time only goes in one direction. Forward. Unless ..." He grinned and took a running leap off the arm of the swing, to arch up high in the air, fold his wings against his back, and dive down into the tall pile of bubbles I had produced. They were slowly disintegrating on the grass between my feet.

Bubbles spattered everywhere, and Maurice arched upward again, trailing streamers of rainbow-tinted drops. He rose higher, to the top bar of the swing, and perched there.

"How about a refill, Lanie?"

"He's going to keep playing at his acrobatic act until you ask him about *unless*," Angela said.

I looked at Kurt and Jane. They just grinned and made a show of wriggling around a little in the evening cool grass to get more comfortable. So I scooped up more bubble solution in the bell of the pipe and took a deep breath and blew, and kept blowing, until I had a mountain of bubbles as high as my knees. They slowly spread out to cover my sneakers and threatened Angela's bare feet. She just chuckled and wiggled her toes and got a chain reaction of popping. Maurice let out a shriek of something that was probably the Fae equivalent of "Geronimo!" and dove, folding his wings flat against his back. Bubbles exploded outward in all directions. He didn't rise up right away, and I had an awful vision for a moment of digging down through the bubbles and finding him splatted flat on the grass, maybe smothered by the bubbles.

We all sat in silence for a few heartbeats, and we exchanged grins that had a little bit of nervousness. Even Angela.

Then Maurice floated up on a huge glob of bubbles, stretched out on his back, with his ankles crossed and a pillow of bubbles propped up his head.

"*Unless* means that someone who comes from a different time stream can go time-diving in your time stream," he announced, and buffed his fingernails on his mint green polo shirt.

"So basically you're volunteering?" Kurt said.

"Volunteering for what?" I had to say.

"I'm just saying," Maurice said, "that it doesn't do you a whole heck of a lot of good to go spying on the past if you can't open the door and walk out and visit. Got any volume control on the thing?"

Chapter Eight

"He's got a point," Jane said. "Anyway, what would we do once we figure out how to call up visions and such? Ask the college to remove all the phone booths from the dorms? Just what we need, kids using a time traveling phone booth to get the answers to exams or trying to make up for not studying or … whatever," she said, and shrugged. Which looked kind of hard to do while lying down. All she really managed to do was nudge Kurt's shoulder.

Then I got an idea, one of those moments when a flash of insight is either brilliance or proof I was losing my mind. I hesitated to share it. Not because I thought they would make fun of me, but because if I was right, we had just wasted a good chunk of time. Maybe all the time Jane and Kurt had put in on trying to activate the time viewing portal or whatever it was the phone booth could do. I thought for a few moments longer, then I had to speak. If just to keep from wasting more time.

"We might have messed ourselves up, coming in from the backside," I said. "What if we were getting the images we wanted, but we couldn't see them because you can only see into the other time, or our memories or whatever the water from Black Pool makes happen, by standing in the hall and looking into the phone booth from that side?"

"And did you ever think that you're not making anything happen because you're not really there to begin with?" Maurice leaped up from the cloud of bubbles, which immediately spun around and plummeted back to the ground, while he hovered there with his wings flapping so fast I could feel the breeze from them. "Jane's all phased out when she uses the Ghost field, so you guys can see and hear what's going on, but you're not really there, there. Know what I mean?"

"Yes, unfortunately, I do," Jane said. In the shadows and the flickers of light from the candles, it was hard to tell, but I suspected she was blushing. Maybe embarrassed that he had figured something out she should have known instinctively about her particular Gift.

We decided to change the angle of the investigation. We would go in during open dorm hours when the only two students on the floor were out all day. We could talk and not use Jane's Ghost field, and no one would hear us or come investigate. We would have the whole floor to ourselves. Maurice agreed to join us, to come at the question from the Fae angle. He warned us that his exile not only shrank his magic, but also limited some things he could do. If the phone booth was in some aspects a dimensional portal, he might not be able to go through. The parameters of the spell controlling his exile kept him from using a lot of doorways that appeared naturally in Divine's Emporium. He also couldn't fold space to travel miles in the matter of a few seconds. He had learned the hard way, when it came to some of the paintings in the fourth floor storage room, he couldn't pass through the dimensional doorways of their frames. Such as when he had pushed Troy Richards, Meggie's brother, when Diane had fallen through a painting. Maurice had wanted to go in to rescue Diane, and had been left behind, scorched. Fortunately, that had worked out. Diane and Troy were an item now, and it looked like we were facing a couple of weddings coming up in Neighborlee.

When I got home, Pete was sitting out on the driveway in a lawn chair, sketching by the light of the driveway floodlight. He gave me a halfhearted little wave and glanced at the kitchen window. There were lights on in the house. I caught shadows, meaning something or someone was moving around inside. I doubted there was enough light for sketching. The really odd detail in this picture was that he had his BB gun leaning against the chair. He waited until I parked my Jeep before he got up and came over to help with my chair.

"Loralee and Cerb are having some kind of meeting." He hooked his thumb over his shoulder toward the house.

"With who? Do I want to even know?"

I had a vision of a whole bunch of dogs of different breeds, sitting around the kitchen table, or maybe the dining room table, drinking out of Mum's fancy teacups and eating powdered sugar tea cakes. Maybe I didn't want to see it, and maybe I did.

We had never asked many questions about the nature of the interdimensional visitors who came to us cloaked in the form of dogs. Maybe the rules and limitations didn't apply to all of them?

The ones assigned to Earth, to observe and help out and report on activities of the rule breakers, were confined to certain physical forms. But what about the ones who came voluntarily, or their superiors, the ones who they reported to? What kind of bodies did they have? Did they have bodies? I thought back to the Star Trek episode with the Organians, who revealed their true shape as these blobby beings of all light and power. Did beings like that even eat tea cakes and drink tea or need to sit at my table?

Of course, that really started to turn my brain into knots, wondering about the implications for Loralee and Cerb's babies, who were currently limited to the shape of puppies. Maurice had even told me that they didn't have much experience with having babies in this current form. I had assumed the dog shape, but what if they meant a physical form, period?

"Are they in trouble, or is this just a checkup for ..." I trailed off when Pete just shrugged. "Did they ask you to get out?"

"Nope. They gave me a note and said they could all fit in the bedroom, but there was all this light spilling through everything, the walls and the vents and whatever, and I had a hard time concentrating on my game, so I came out here. It's like there wasn't enough room to breathe, they just ... you know ... they kind of take up all the space."

"Okay ..."

I considered getting back into my Jeep and heading over to Divine's to ask some advice on this. My arms were tired and I just did not want to go anywhere, much less load my chair back into the back seat, drive over there, get my chair out again, and have to navigate getting into the shop. Angela and Maurice had probably gone inside by now. It was late. And I was just plain tired.

Of course, there was the question of when I could go into my own house. I really needed to think a little longer next time an interdimensional being that wasn't even wearing her own body asked if she could spend her pregnancy in my spare bedroom.

Pete settled down again and I pulled up close enough to check out his sketchpad. He was working on some illustrations for the next fanzine our Trek club was going to publish in the fall. I saw the BB gun, now leaning against the ramp. Pete blushed hard enough to be visible in the low light.

"I thought I saw something creeping around in the trees. I

could have sworn it was more of those freaky dwarf faerie things."

"The lawn gnomes?" I shivered a little when he nodded. "Did you shoot any of them?"

"Took a couple shots. Not sure I hit anything."

I clasped my hands under my chin and fluttered my eyelashes. "My hero."

Pete snorted.

The light in the kitchen flared a little brighter, and I flinched, wondering if Cerb and Loralee's superiors had maybe heard me thinking my questions, and silently grumbling. Then it went out. There was a faint glow, and I thought maybe it was the nightlight in the corner, left on to help people in search of midnight snacks -- Pete -- avoid stubbing his big feet on chairs or the sides of cabinets when he got up and navigated with one eye open.

The back door opened. No one came out. I counted to twenty. Then started over and counted to fifty. Then I had an awful vision of mosquitoes and other night critters flying in through that open door, drawn by the night light. Sighing, I grabbed hold of my wheels and gave a good hard shove to cross the driveway to the end of the ramp. Pete didn't say anything. I heard the creak of the lawn chair folding up as he put it away in the little plastic storage shed on the side of the garage. I looked back when I got to the back door, and he was just starting up the ramp.

If the guests had helped themselves to anything, there was no evidence. I wheeled through the kitchen and down the hall to the bedroom Loralee and Cerb had been using.

Had been. Past tense. Because everything was put back the way it had been when Maurice first brought them to my door. The hardwood floor had even been dusted. No dog hair. The drawers used as stairs to get from the floor to the bed had been pushed in. The linens were clean and folded, and there was a smell of laundry fresh from the dryer filling the room. Wow, nice, considerate guests. And that included what turned out to be a thank-you note, left on the mattress next to the folded sheets.

I couldn't read it, of course. The writing was this mixture of swoopy and jagged marks in pale blue ink on ivory paper. At least, I thought it was ink and paper. Forget about the language, I couldn't even decipher the alphabet. I took the note with me when I met Jane and Maurice and Kurt in the back parking lot by the dorm the next morning.

Maurice had me spread the note out on the floor once we got up to the third floor and made sure we really were alone. He walked along it, back and forth a couple times, and I had the feeling he was having a hard time reading the note.

"Okay, basically there's been some big change in their government, Loralee is now so close to the throne or a chance to sit on the throne, or what passes for a throne, she's been taken out of the field. No more work for her, she's overseeing things. And the babies are too royal to be born out in the field, so they all got taken back home. Everything's good and ..." He took a deep breath. "There's a bunch of high-power folks who owe you big-time. I can't even interpret all the fine print, the conditions when you can claim the favors or help or whatever, but a lot of people like you. And there's a warning that some people who owe you aren't too happy about owing you, so maybe it's not a good thing to claim that favor unless you're really, really, like end of the world desperate."

"Huh. You got all that out of a handful of squiggles and slash marks?" Kurt said. He nudged the note with the toe of his boot.

Jane laughed. "Every single line is a couple pages of explanation crammed in. You have to magnify your vision a couple hundred times to get it all." She held out her hand to him. "Want me to show you?"

He looked at it, cocked an eyebrow at her, then took a step back. "Thanks, I'll take your word for it." Then he grinned. "I bet Felicity is going to be kind of ticked that she never got in on this."

"She's too busy being a disgustingly happy newlywed. Besides, she couldn't hear Cerb like she could hear normal dogs." I reached with my mind, folded up the note and tugged it up off the floor, into my hand. A few seconds later I had it folded up, back into the protective packet in my backpack. "What do you want to do first with the phone booth problem?"

We opened it and found another inch of swirling, misty-dark streaked water collected in the bottom. This was after the phone booth had been mopped dry and sprayed with disinfecting spray for good measure just this morning. We just stood or sat there and looked at the water, or whatever it was. How had it gotten there? None of us really wanted to touch it.

In that silence, we heard a soft *plink-splash*. A drop of water had fallen.

"Okay, that helps," Kurt muttered. He pulled open the backpack with some basic gear he had brought, took out his big, blocky, knock-em-out-with-one-blow flashlight and set it up on the floor. The case had one of those enormous giga-volt square batteries, with the light on a pivot, so he could turn it to shine at any angle. He set the flashlight down on the floor and focused the beam across the surface of the water, and waited.

Just a few seconds later, another drop. This time Kurt caught the ripples in the water from the drop. He located the center of the ripples and slowly swept the beam upward, muttered something, then got down on the floor and looked up.

"Huh. Kind of explains things. And gives us another mystery." He gestured at the wooden triangle seat that filled one corner of the phone booth.

Maurice flew into the phone booth and hovered under the seat, with the flashlight beam sparkling off his wings. "Okay, I see. Yeah, weird." He let out a yelp and darted back out, narrowly missing getting hit with a huge drop of water. "There's a whole bunch of drops forming on the bottom side of the seat. Looks like they're just coming through the wood."

"Okay, Ming was sitting on that seat in her wet bathing suit, talking on the phone for hours, according to Rita," I said, thinking aloud. "Water soaked into the wood. Collected there. Maybe never really dried. Especially if the phone booth was closed up all the time. Maybe enough weird, enhanced water filled the wood, soaked in, it … what? Changed the composition of the seat, made the wood into a doorway? Created a channel between Black Water and the phone booth?"

"I've seen weirder." Maurice shrugged. Somehow, it wasn't as funny this time when that gesture jerked him sideways in the air.

"Then explain the link between Jinx's pond and Black Water," Kurt said.

Jane volunteered to go down and talk to Rita. She found out yes, Ming and her life sciences project team had gone into Jinx's pond, too, even though that area was posted as off-limits. The park rangers overseeing the activity at Black Water should have seen when some students went off and did some exploring and taking water samples from other areas in the park without permission.

Ming fell into Jinx's pond when she was collecting samples from different areas and levels, using a long rod with a sealed container on the end and a simple trigger to open and close it. She had felt a little sick, probably from swallowing water, and went back to the dorm early. The students didn't report the incident because they shouldn't have been there in the first place. Ming didn't go to the hospital or the college health center because she didn't want to get everyone in the project in trouble. Rita only knew about it because she heard Ming arguing with several other girls on the project.

Then, feeling kind of dizzy and nauseated, Ming decided the *smart* thing to do was sit in the phone booth for hours, in her wet clothes, talking with her boyfriend? That enabled the water-not-water to soak from her bathing suit into the wooden seat of the phone booth.

It combined with the water from Black Water Pool that she had been leaving there all along.

Honestly, didn't she pick up anything, any of the rules of survival, that sort of sank in and affected the subconscious of anyone who managed to last more than one year at Willis-Brooks College? She was a science student, for heaven's sake. Shouldn't that have guaranteed a little higher intelligence? Well, maybe intelligence, but not wisdom. The goofballs on *Big Bang Theory* and other shows about higher-than-average intelligent people certainly taught that intellectual geniuses didn't have much in the way of common sense. Like street smarts, and survival skills.

Ming and the rest of the science project team should have had the sense God gave birds, at the very least, to raise their hands and say, "Excuse me, I think we did something stupid, could we have some help here?"

I checked with Angela while we were waiting for Rita to get that information for us. Angela said Ming had come into Divine's only a handful of times in the three years she had been at WB. She hadn't seen her at all that summer.

So the question we came up with was a little darker and more troubling: Had Ming come under the influence of some outside force trying to cause trouble? Had her fall into Jinx's pond not been an accident? Was the link between the two pools an attempt to cause trouble? Or just one of those freaky coincidences that couldn't be called luck, either good or bad? But they couldn't be called deliberate or even (perhaps this was blasphemy?) answers to really stupid prayers. I'm talking the kind that God answers yes, just to teach us to pay better attention to the things we ask for, nag Him for. Honestly, even after how the whole mess turned out, I wasn't sure who to blame or thank for what happened. Maybe a lot of different people?

We operated on the theory that some link had been forged between Black Water and Jinx's pond, and created some kind of dimensional doorway that opened into the phone booth.

We confiscated a bunch of towels that had been abandoned over the school year and left in the lost-and-found. This required another trip by Jane, using the Ghost field to fly invisibly up and down the stairs. We mopped up and dried up the floor of the phone booth. Then we washed it down with the neutralizer solution Angela had sent along with Maurice. Kurt had a pair of waterproof gloves. He wadded up a towel directly under the phone booth seat, to catch the water that would keep coming through the wood. Then he proved how brave he was, and how careful he was. He put on a pair of goggles, the staple of school shop classes the world over, lay on his back, and proceeded to remove the wooden seat from the phone booth. Or at least, he tried.

"Hey, gang, do we want to do that?" Maurice said, when Kurt gave up trying to get the first screw out with a normal screwdriver, and asked Jane to hand him his Yankee screwdriver.

"What do you mean?" Kurt grunted with the effort as he pushed on the handle of the screwdriver for the first time.

He was pushing up, since he was working upside down. The metal protested. I wasn't sure for a few seconds if that screech came from the screwdriver's gears and ratchets or whatever it was that put extra power into the turning action. Maybe that protest came from the stubborn screw, or the metal side of the phone booth that didn't want to let go of it.

"Well, we didn't find out if we could time travel coming from the outside. What if removing the seat turns it off?" Maurice said.

"That's a good thing," I said. "You do not want to leave a door to another dimension in a college dorm. Just think what those kids could do with something that lets them travel through time. Imagine kids studying for a history test, going back to see some big battle in person, and either getting themselves killed or changing history."

"Rules of space and time," he said, flying out of the phone booth to hover in front of me. "Time goes only one direction. Forward."

"*Unless*, like you said." Jane waved a finger at him. "Some people in this town have Fae blood. What if they don't have to be living, or having had lived, in a different time stream? What if they step into this phone booth and figure out how to change their place in the time stream of Earth because their Fae blood is strong enough to anchor them in the Fae time stream?"

"It's not that simple." His voice softened, and even though his face was so small, I had the feeling Maurice wasn't as certain as he wanted to be. Maybe he was getting ideas or at least warning visions of possible trouble.

Meanwhile, Kurt had been pounding away with the Yankee screwdriver and forcing those screws out from the bar that supported and connected the wooden seat to the corner of the phone booth. Each push earned a metallic scream of protest. Four screws on each side. He was sweating by the time he handed the eighth screw to Jane, then slid out of the phone booth far enough he could sit up without hitting his head on the seat. He turned over, got on his knees, and put a hand on the top of the seat and pushed. Nothing moved. He pushed a little harder.

The metal corner bar that supported the seat fell down with a *clatter-clang* and echoes that made us all flinch. It certainly seemed loud enough, in the quiet of that hallway, I wouldn't have been surprised if the sound rang all the way down to the first floor.

The wooden triangle of the seat stayed in place, even with nothing to support it.

"That just ain't right," Kurt muttered. Then he grinned. "Screwdriver -- flathead." He held out his hand and Jane dug into his backpack until she found it. He wedged it in maybe half an inch deep, between the seat and the wall. He tried to lever it free. In five different places. No luck.

"That thing really wants to stay here," Maurice said.

"I don't know," Jane said with a shrug and a lopsided grin for us. "Maybe it's time for an exorcism? Maybe we should soak it in holy water?"

"Why not?" Kurt got that crooked grin. "Got any more of

Angela's neutralizer?"

He poured the rest of the container on the top of the seat, focusing on getting it in the crack between seat and wall, then took another abandoned towel and wiped down the still-dripping underside.

Good news: the dripping stopped.

Bad news: the seat still didn't come free.

We ended up flying to Divine's, discussing the situation with Angela for an hour, then we split up. I had to go to work. Fortunately, it was a paper delivery day, so I had just flipped my usual schedule and worked my half day in the afternoon instead of the morning. Jane had a spa to run. So it was left up to Kurt to go back to the dorm with a big batch of Angela's neutralizer, and instructions for Rita to keep wiping down the seat whenever she noticed it was dripping. Hopefully, the neutralizer would stop the dripping eventually, or maybe even destroy whatever attached the wooden seat to the metal wall, and it would fall free. Eventually. The "fun" thing about the kind of magic we dealt with in Neighborlee? There was often no way to predict what would work and what would happen in reaction to the things we tried.

~~~~~

Stanzer called to tell us that he had found the old nursing home. A Hound was keeping him company and blocking him from even trying to penetrate the low-key security. Meaning the Feds were guarding someone and didn't want the locals to be suspicious or even aware. Meaning whoever they were guarding faced a real threat. That made sense. The girl who survived that car chase, gun battle and blue lightning strike was the only witness. If the FBI thought she knew where the stolen information had been hidden, then that crime boss Archby probably thought so too.

London and Sherwood did more work researching Archby. They dug and kept coming up against firewalls and the equivalent of trip wires and alarms. Archby probably had some computer geniuses working for him, protecting his organization's files and trying to hide his presence online.

Athena, Wallace, and Cosmo were working on tracking down the actions of the agent and the team working against Archby, and trying to identify the other four young people who had been killed. Athena got a good image of the Cedar Point tickets and had tracked
~~~~~

them down to a batch sold to a grocery store chain in southern Ohio. The stores didn't keep records of which tickets were sold to which credit card. It was taking a while to get into the electronic receipts of the chain to try to match up a purchase of five tickets to who might have bought them for that weekend trip to Cedar Point that had never happened. Five tickets together in one envelope in the glove compartment of the truck meant someone had bought all five at the same time, rather than each person in the group buying their own tickets. Maybe these tickets came from a larger group, like for an organization that then distributed tickets to their members.

Wallace was searching the police departments for the surrounding communities, looking for reports of a group of teens who had gone missing. Certainly by now, there should be someone raising an alarm when their kids didn't come home.

~~~~~

Thursday, Stanzer called me at work to tell me he had touched the consciousness of the girl in his dreams. That was good news. Except that she seemed to be confused, unable to reach out or respond to him. He had the impression that it wasn't so much that the Hound was blocking their connection, but the girl hadn't been able to participate in mental communication until then. He was worried that she was so injured, she was unable to use whatever talent she had inherited from her bloodline. If she was as young as the accident report estimated, then maybe she didn't know she had a Gift. Maybe she didn't know or remember anything about the Hunt.

"That kind of explains why the Hound reacted like it did, when it protected her," Stanzer said before he hung up, to let me get back to work. "They work in harmony with us. They aren't really our servants, but they react to what we ask of them. She didn't know what to ask, she just instinctively called a Hound in a moment of panic or terror."

"At least her mind is working enough for you to make that contact," I offered. Yeah, as if I knew anything about telepathic communication? Everything I "knew" was all theorizing, learned from reading science fiction and fantasy, not experience. Not like the training Jane had received growing up.

I emailed Stanzer right after we hung up, with ideas I couldn't
~~~~~

say over the phone, just in case anyone overheard me. I suggested he call Daniel's mother and grandmother. They were the ones with healing gifts and experience. Or he could talk to Jane and maybe have her direct him to someone at Hoax who could give him information or guidance. Or maybe even join him in Sandusky and try to get through all that security. Maybe super-fast Katie could zip in, pick up the girl, and zip out again, without the security cameras catching her. They might need to get her out of there and into the hands of someone who could heal her. At the very least, he might need the assistance of someone with more skill, to make contact with the girl if she wasn't healing, wasn't able to participate in any closer or more coherent contact.

Rita called me that afternoon with what we hoped was good news -- the phone booth seat had fallen loose when she was applying the twice daily treatment of neutralizer. She wasn't about to risk touching it. She had doused it with more neutralizer and called me to send someone to come get the seat out of the dorm. No one had used the phone booth since Ming left at the end of first summer term, and they probably wouldn't use it when the fall semester started. These modern kids all had cell phones and didn't need landline phones or campus phones. If we were lucky, no one would notice the seat was missing until next school year.

Chapter Nine

When I called Kurt, I found out he and Ford Longfellow and Jinx and Jane had been taking turns observing Black Water Pool and Jinx's pond. They wanted to be ready to catch any response or effect from the neutralizer soaking into the phone booth seat. Especially when the link between the two bodies of water broke.

Kurt and Jane were having a picnic at the top of the cliff overlooking Black Water when the seat fell, and they reported no reaction. Jinx was on duty at his pond and thought maybe he did see a flicker of something. He wasn't sure. It was a sunny afternoon.

Kurt and Jane flew up to the dorm floor and entered using the Ghost field. They brought a heavy-duty plastic zipper bag full of neutralizer, and big ice tongs. It was a matter of two minutes to pick up the seat, put it in the bag, seal it, then fly out, with no witnesses. They took it to Angela to deal with. She and Maurice had arrangements ready in one of the sub-cellars at Divine's. Essentially, they were going to let the seat drip dry, sitting on a wire rack, with space heaters going full blast to avoid something nasty like magically enhanced mold growing on it. When the seat had entirely dried, then they would test it and see if there was any link between the two bodies of water.

~~~~~

"Anybody else curious what would happen if we combined water from both pools directly?" Kurt said, after a meeting of the guardians on Friday night.

Athena, Wallace, and London had reported what they had found out so far. The VIN plate and license plates for the truck the five young people had been in had been destroyed in the explosion. Tracking down the ownership of the truck through serial numbers on the parts might also be impossible, depending on the damage. The government agents were also following the clue of the Cedar Point tickets, but not as quickly as we had. We debated the possible problems if we tried to "nudge" the Feds in the right direction. Would we just be muddying the waters, putting the agents on alert that someone had infiltrated their security, and maybe distract
~~~~~

them from the more important investigation?

Wallace had determined there were several summer camps in the general radius of the grocery store chain that had sold the tickets. We had some hope for about ten seconds. Then he reported that all the camps had bought blocks of tickets, some as many as 100 in a unit. We were back to the beginning, because how could we identify five specific tickets that hadn't been used from those big blocks, until the end of the summer? By then, it would be too late. Wallace was searching for which camps had reported missing campers. Maybe camp staffers, enjoying their weekend off between camping sessions?

There was little else we could do to help Stanzer until the injured girl could make more coherent contact with him in their dreams, or the Hound that accompanied him allowed him to approach the building. What would happen when he did that? Would the agents protecting the girl allow him to talk to her? Stanzer had talked to Angela that morning, reporting on his dreams and getting what little information Athena and Wallace had gathered. He confessed that the Hound could help him walk through walls, if necessary. The operative word was "could." His father had warned him about proper behavior and attitude toward the Hounds, when the Hunt was given to them to be taken to safety. Acting foolishly, selfishly, violating vows and honor, could result in forfeiting all help from the Hounds. If they didn't agree with Stanzer's actions, they could refuse to help at the worst possible time, essentially letting him suffer for his bad choices.

All we could do was prepare to run to help him when or if he called, and pray.

So we focused on our own mysteries and possibilities.

I really wished we had something else to think about. But Loralee and Cerb were gone, with no word when the puppies/babies would be born, or if they had already been born. Without any new holes being dug in my yard, either by dog or by intruders, I had the boring, irritating task of putting my lawn back together.

So we were left with nothing to do but gnaw on the question of what the people from Pi Surprise wanted with Emma's beads, when the lawn gnomes would try to sneak up on my house again, and the magical properties of Black Water and Jinx's pond.

Obviously, from his remark, Kurt preferred that last topic.

"Curiosity killed the cat," Jane murmured, with a wink for me and her head carefully turned so Kurt didn't see.

He seemed to see anyway. Funny, but if I had been teasing him he would have sighed or gotten irritated. He just smirked at Jane behind her back. She seemed to see or at least sense it. I wasn't sure if their growing mental unity was cute, irritating, or if it would get a little creepy after too much of it.

"What do you suggest we do?" Ford glanced first at Jinx on his right, then Athena on his left. "I've got this image in my head of the equivalent of a nuclear blast, if we do something stupid like dumping a couple bucketsful of water from one into the other."

I shuddered, the image all too clear in my head now, too.

"Start small," Kurt said. "Use one of those places out at the quarries where the rock is pretty solid, not porous, where the water collects when it rains. Start out small, just a cup of each at a time, kind of poured into neutral territory."

"You've been thinking about this for a while," Angela said.

"He's been calling the mad scientists at Hoax, having highly philosophical discussions," Jane said. "Sometimes I think he's been talking to them more than to me."

"And that's a problem for you because?" Kurt shot back.

We all laughed. I muffled a sigh that I was afraid might be jealousy. Jane was so good for him, and he seemed to make her happy, so I was glad for them. But I wanted that, too.

We discussed the water mystery for a while, and gradually we all agreed, yes, we were a little curious.

This was one of those situations where precautions were necessary, even though it got a little tricky deciding what to tell the authorities and anticipating their reactions. Jinx, fortunately, had a couple friends among the park rangers. That was how he and Ford were able to camp out at his pond. Jinx told them we were experimenting with water drawn from the pond, and where we were planning to work in the quarries. The spot had been carefully chosen, where no one would interfere with us and no one would be close enough to be hurt if anything went wrong.

Notice I said he *told* his ranger friends, rather than *asked permission*? The rangers trusted Jinx enough that they didn't get offended. They also didn't ask questions. They probably would have, if they had known we were bringing water from Black Water Pool. Of course, Black Water wasn't really off-limits or under observation. Not like Jinx's pond. Still, it had a reputation.

That was just another example of how the ever-present background weirdness and magic of Neighborlee just made it easier for us to get away with stunts that anywhere else would have had people putting on the brakes. Maybe filing injunctions to stop us doing what we were doing. Or at the very least shouting, "Stop! Don't be stupid!"

Then again, what we wanted to do wouldn't be possible anywhere else. So kind of a moot point.

Saturday morning, we gathered in the quarries. There were quite a few of us, observers as well as those conducting the experiment. I had been keeping Daniel and his grandfather updated on what we were doing. Daniel was still out of town on business, but Arthur and Daniel's mother, Annamarie came. Demetrius and Beau at Hoax were interested, but couldn't join us. Everyone came armed with their smartphones to take pictures and video. Angela came with a large bottle of neutralizer. There was something unnervingly prosaic about the fact she brought it in an old two-liter ginger ale bottle, instead of something more appropriate to magical elements. Like a fire-darkened leather bucket or a copper urn or something like that. She also might have laughed at me if I spoke my thoughts.

Ford and Jinx brought four one-gallon milk jugs of water from Jinx's pond. Kurt and Jane brought a half-dozen two-liter bottles, carefully retrieved from different depths of Black Water Pool, and labeled to keep them separate. Kurt was really getting into this experiment.

We set up in one of the lower levels of the quarries, an area that was open to the public. We would have preferred something that would have made it harder for some innocent, curious passersby to wander in and see something they shouldn't. The rock we needed determined the location for the experiment. We wanted something that wouldn't let the water soak through and trickle down and away too quickly, if at all. We also had to try to keep away from the natural path of water in the quarries, so it wouldn't feed into pool or pond. If there was some reaction when the water of the two merged in any quantity, we didn't want to add to the explosion.

The way we had it figured, the water would go into the river and be diluted before it joined the water table of the Metroparks.

Maybe I should have called Pastor Rocky, and asked for some prayers to cover any backwash from our experiment?

When we were all gathered together, we spent some time discussing exactly how we were going to conduct this semi-scientific experiment in magic. We did have to plan our steps and details, such as how much of each kind of water we would pour into the basin in the rock, in what order, that sort of thing. Then Gordon asked a really smart question.

"Do we have to do it here?" He gestured around. "Does it have to be a hole in the rock? I mean, what if we used like a plastic bowl, or glass, or metal?" He shrugged and gave us a crooked little grin, like he expected to be laughed at any second now.

Angela patted Gordon's shoulder. "There is far more guardian in you than any of us thought. Indeed, distance from the sources might help us. Protect us, at the very least."

"And might make sure nothing works at all," Kurt pointed out. "Then again, maybe we don't want it to work."

"Says the guy who's been scribbling all sorts of diagrams for a time travel machine powered by magical water," Jane said in a sing-song voice, looking upward as if she was talking to a couple of birds gliding past far overhead.

The rest of us laughed.

In the end, we agreed we'd conduct a few steps of the experiment right there, since we had gone to all the trouble of hauling the water and meeting there. If something big happened, or if nothing happened, we would need to test conditions and make sure that the rock of the quarries wasn't somehow involved in the time traveling visions mess. We would then conduct the experiment in different places in town, and outside town, using plastic, glass and metal bowls. Just to be scientific.

We started with a cup of each water poured into the shallowest dip in the rock at the same time. Then added a cup of each, alternating, from Jinx's pond, then Black Water. Then another cup, with Black Water first, then Jinx's pond. By that time, the water was almost level with the top of the dip in the rock. Nothing happened with the water.

We moved to another bowl in the rock, but tried to keep an eye on the first, to see if there was any delayed reaction, and measure how fast the water soaked into the rock and drained away.

"Look!" Daniel's mother, Annamarie skidded a little in her hurry to go back to the first shallow depression in the rock.

I turned my chair around just in time to get a soft flash of light, kind of a shimmer of rainbow.

When we went back to the bowl in the rock, it was empty. Dry. Not even damp.

Of course, we didn't pay attention to the exact moment when we put the water in, so we could only guess how long it took to flash and -- what? -- teleport out, or just hyper-fast evaporate? Maybe ten minutes, for about four cups of water.

"I propose we try to be as scientific as possible," Arthur said. He pulled a small notepad out of his back pocket.

It turned out we didn't need to add more water to get a reaction in the second depression in the rock, we just had to wait. At three minutes, the shimmer started, swirling around in the center of the depression. Kurt scooped up water from one container and gestured for Jane to get the measuring cup for the other container. They trickled water into the depression, and the shimmer died away. A glance to Arthur, and he tapped the timer on his smartphone. The shimmer began at eight minutes. So, the more water we put in, maybe the longer it took for the reaction?

When we ran out of room in the second bowl, we moved to the largest depression in the plateau, while keeping the timer going on the first one.

We experimented, adding more water, in different orders, and recorded how much longer it took after each infusion of water for the shimmer to start up.

Finally, we ran out of water in the containers and eventually it all shimmered and vanished. So, what did we learn? Besides the water taking longer to generate light and vanish in geometric proportion to how much we put into a bowl in the rock.

We thought too late about putting something in the water, to see if it would be taken away when the water vanished. Of course, how could we know where the water went?

"I could put together a simple little camera with a battery. Or a GPS would be a good idea," Kurt said, thinking aloud, when Annamarie asked that question.

"This has been fun, and fascinating, and a little frightening." Arthur took one more glance at the sheets of data he had written down, closed his notebook, and put it back in his pocket. "But what good does all this do us? It isn't like we can control the process."

"Knowing how to predict when something will happen is a step toward control," Ford offered. His eyes narrowed and he tipped his head to one side as he looked at Kurt. "Did you feel anything?" He rubbed his fingertips together on one hand, our signal for the vibrations of energy that Kurt felt when semi-pseudo-superheroes used their Gifts.

"Like, if I feel what's going on, maybe I can access it, put some controls on it?" Kurt shook his head. "Not a thing. I'm not getting anything more than the rest of you do. Just the light show."

"And no visions," Angela murmured. "How did you manage to get that image from Trick-or-Treating as children?"

"I'm going to be a little ticked if we find out the wood in the seat is an important part," I said. "Or maybe the glass in the phone booth. Or maybe the entire phone booth. Maybe it picked up some weirdness from that whole mess my freshman year."

"Think we can steal the whole phone booth?" Kurt said, waggling his eyebrows at Jane. She just sighed and shook her head.

"Save that for later," Jinx said. "I'd like to see you do it, though." He frowned, looking down at the now-dry depression in the stone. "How come we didn't see anything? How did you get the vision the first time?"

"We weren't trying," I said. "There was a smell that reminded all of us of that Halloween, and then we were thinking or remembering …"

Angela laughed.

"Ask and ye shall receive," she said.

"We didn't ask, we didn't even try … can it be that easy? Focus on what we *want* to see, and we get it?"

"We won't know until we try."

"Next time, I want to see what happens if we throw a couple gallons of Black Water into Jinx's pond," Kurt said.

"Later," Angela said, shaking her head, with that little smirk that either meant she knew Kurt was joking, or warned him if he wasn't joking. "Much later. Baby steps, please."

~~~~~
~~~~~

Kurt and Jane stopped at Divine's and checked the wooden seat taken from the phone booth, to see if it was receiving any water or doing anything bizarre. Either removing the last of the moisture had permanently severed the connection, or something had happened, but left no residue or indication. He called to let me know what they had found (nothing), and we agreed that next time we did an experiment with the two waters, we would have someone posted to watch the seat. The question was who would have to sit in the back room of Divine's, keeping an eye on a triangle of old wood, and miss out on whatever weird reaction we got the next time.

~~~~~

Over dinner, I told Harry and Pete what we had done at the quarries, and then proposed a theory that had been germinating all day while I was busy with other things, like my *Terry* column and business for our Trek club. Between all the reading they did, the online discussion groups they belonged to, and podcasts they listened to, especially the ones that tried to make science fiction science a reality, my brothers might have some better ideas than me. Especially a better idea if what I proposed was totally off base, or possible, or could open doors to trouble.

We discussed that moment in the dorm hall when Col. Hayward, Kurt and I all shared a memory. I went back in my mind and tried to find anything in the dorm hall that might have triggered that shared memory, so we all focused on one specific time in the past, without realizing it. And I found it. The bulletin board next to the phone booth still had flyers and announcements left over from the last school year. Specifically, the announcement for the community Halloween party, asking for volunteers to help, in the partnership between the college and the town.

If something so vague could trigger a shared memory between us, what would happen if three of us focused, with a strong emotional element, on something we wanted to see?

Like … our parents?

This coming fall would be two years since they took off on their research trip. Hayward had gathered up all the data the government investigators and unofficial watchers had compiled, relating to weather and energy emissions and other meteorological events leading up to Mum and Pop's arrival in Bermuda. Anything
~~~~~

that had happened, whether noteworthy or not, during the time they were seen wandering the island. Anything that happened, electrical, chemical, meteorological, even incidents with tourists, in the month before and the month after they vanished. London and Sherwood had found a few bits and pieces that might be helpful, that hadn't been in any of the reports. Things that had either escaped the notice of the government investigators or had been ignored because it was deemed as having no connection with the disappearance.

We had all the information that could possibly be gathered, but none of it did us any good. So maybe our folks vanished because of something totally bizarre, something nobody had seen because nobody was watching when it happened? So what if we were able to find them and watch them, until it, whatever it was, happened?

We decided to make this first attempt just between the three of us. Honestly, I might have tried it by myself, to protect the boys, but I needed their help getting the water, and rolling my wheelchair from the parking lot to the plateau where we had been experimenting. I figured, even if we didn't detect any water remaining in the depressions in the rock, some other residue could have built up. For what I wanted to do, I needed all the help I could get.

Let me say right here, I did not expect what we managed to do, but I did hope for something close to it.

We didn't tell anybody what we were doing, in case our theories didn't work, and all we ended up with was another light show. We were taking a big chance on getting caught by the wrong park ranger checking out the quarries at the wrong time. We didn't want sympathy, and we didn't want other people's memories of our folks to interfere with the reception, so to speak.

Most important of all, if we were looking into the past, we hoped to get some information, not just a glimpse of the last memory we had of our parents: the image from the DVD they sent us, that reached us on Christmas Eve.

We had no idea if we could control whatever happened tonight. If anything happened. All we could do was try. Like Pop was always telling us, God didn't ask us to succeed, all He asked was that we would try.

So there we were, past 10 on a warm summer evening. We had

a couple blankets spread on the bare rock of the plateau, so I could get out of my chair and present as small a profile as possible in case anyone came by on patrol. I was ready with my smartphone camera. Just in case, I was ready to switch it to video. Who knows? Maybe there would be sound that came with the picture? Maybe we could talk through time with our folks? But that begged the question: If we could talk through time, *should we?* Would we tear a hole in the space-time continuum if we warned our folks something was about to happen? Even if we didn't know exactly what was going to happen? Would warning them make the disappearance happen? Like all those people in mythology who were given a terrible prophecy and in trying to avert it brought it about? Anticipating trouble was draining our energy. Asking questions about things that might never happen was wasting time.

"Ready?" Harry asked. He was on his knees to the right of the biggest basin in the rock, with the Black Water Pool water. Pete was on the left with the water from Jinx's pond.

I nodded. I picked up the printouts Pete had made from the last image on the DVD, of our parents sitting on the beach in Bermuda. Pop in his ugly shorts and hairy legs, and Mum in her bikini, both of them smiling at us.

As agreed, the boys poured water into the basin, one cup at a time, simultaneously. When the basin was full, five cups of each, they scooted around to kneel or sit cross-legged on the blanket with me. I handed them their copies of the picture, and we focused on it. Every few seconds, I looked up and studied the water.

Much sooner than I expected it, with so much water in the basin, that shimmering light popped into being in the middle of the water. Okay, one theory proven: focused thought, agreeing on what we wanted to see, did have some effect. I choked back a little laughter at how much time we had wasted that morning. Still, if our theories were correct, we might not have seen anything anyway, because we wouldn't have been agreeing on what we wanted to see. Between my brothers and me, we could guarantee a lot of emotional energy invested in the effort.

"Do you smell something?" Pete whispered.

I sniffed, and a second later realized just how stupid that reaction was. Even though teaming up with Hoax and the Sheridan group last year had resulted in dealing some very big, damaging blows to the Rivals, there was no guarantee there weren't some cells or pocket groups still out there, and gunning for us. We were playing right into their hands, coming out here late at night with no backup. How hard would it be for them to spray us with the same sleeping gas or nerve gas they had used on Hayward and the two boys two winters ago? How fast would the gas work? Too fast for me to call for help? I tapped my phone, ready to type in the password and hit speed dial.

Then I caught what Pete smelled. That tang in the air. Something fresh. Salty? Fruity?

"Coconut tanning oil," Harry said, and snorted. "Any sun bathers out here today?"

"Saltwater?" I said, keeping my voice down, just in case.

And in those few seconds of confusion, the light spread out from the tiny seed in the middle of the water, to fill the entire bowl.

A warm breeze that did not smell anything like the usual damp and stone and moss of the quarries brushed past us. It smelled of the ocean, salt and seaweed, and sun on sand.

I muffled a yelp as the light in the water took on color and I recognize that shade of green before it resolved into Mum's hair. Then the other colors clarified and brightened and turned into that awful orange of Pop's Bermuda shorts, and the yellow of Mum's bikini. And the deep blue of the water and the white of the sand around them.

They smiled at us, and waved, and just like in those last few seconds of the DVD, Mum raised her hand and squeezed the little black box of the remote control for the video camera. This time, instead of the image freezing or dying completely, Mum leaned into Pop and rested her head on his shoulder. He wrapped his arm tighter around her and his mouth moved, but we didn't hear anything.

"No sound, but the extended director's cut, at least." Harry grinned at us. I caught it from the corner of my eye, because I was not taking my gaze off our parents for anything.

"We get smells, but not sound," Pete whispered. "Doesn't seem fair."

Sound or no sound, I wasn't going to waste this. I fumbled with my phone to turn on the video, and held it up where I could record the image in the water, but not interfere with seeing the image itself.

Pop pressed a kiss to Mum's forehead. They got up off the blanket, moving kind of slow, almost like they were feeling their years. That chilled me a little bit. Maybe I was just reading things into the images that weren't really there?

The image followed Mum and Pop as he folded up the blanket and retrieved their shoes, which were under the tripod for the video camera. Mum stowed the camera and compacted the tripod and put them in their case. Pop took the case from her and put it over his shoulder while she put on a beach wrap, then he wrapped his free arm around her waist, and they set off down the beach.

I checked my watch, half-terrified something important would happen in the image while my gaze was off it. Mum and Pop continued walking, completely relaxed. Two minutes had passed since the speck of light first appeared in the water.

We watched them pass people, who were coming down to the beach and spreading blankets and chairs and setting up umbrellas, preparing for their day of relaxing in the sun. We muffled laughter a few times, when we got good views of the faces of some of the people after our folks passed, and they reacted to what they had seen. Either Pop's long gray-white ponytail or his ugly orange Bermuda shorts had started them, a combination of the two, or the curvy Asian woman with long green hair. Take your pick. Gee, with all the tattoos and body piercings and bizarre hair color we saw among the people coming down to the water in what passed for swimwear, yet wouldn't provide enough cloth to use as a dishrag, why were people giving *them* odd looks? Maybe because our folks were rather sedate, compared to a lot of the sun worshippers and beach bums increasing in numbers around them?

I hoped we could discuss this morning with our folks someday.

Chapter Ten

Eventually Mum and Pop made their way off the beach and onto a long promenade area, with shops on the far edge of the paved area, facing the beach. They strolled along, stopping at a food cart to get drinks with what looked like a long stick of pineapple in each squat cup. Then at another cart got some kind of bread pocket. Judging from the angle of the shadows stretching out long behind them, it was early morning, and they were on the western side of the island. I whispered that deduction. Harry wrote it down, nodding agreement.

We looked for signs that might indicate a street, or at least a store we could refer to, some information we could give to Athena and Wallace, maybe pass on to London to do some more digging. The chances were almost nil that a beachside shop or even the local police would have video records from security cameras from nearly two years before, but we wouldn't know until we asked.

The image bobbed around Mum and Pop, like the camera was hanging from a drone operated by an antsy three-year-old. It hung in front of them, then alongside them. Then followed them for a couple dozen steps, then veered off to look at whatever cart they had stopped to look at. Or swerved into a shop selling all sorts of touristy trinkets or beach gear. It never focused on their faces long enough to suit me. I really wished one of us had learned lip-reading, so we could understand what they were talking about, maybe get a clue to what was on their minds that day.

As near as we could figure, between the date on the video, the postal date on the envelope the DVD arrived in, and when the hotel reported them missing, this was just one or at the most four days before Mum and Pop vanished.

It took him about eight months, but Hayward had retrieved our folks' belongings from their hotel. Either someone had stolen vital clues without leaving any hint that the hotel room had been robbed, or Mum and Pop hadn't left any clues behind them. Maybe their important notes were with them when they vanished. Or got sucked into a vortex. Or got kidnapped by aliens. Or got snatched by agents of the Rivals, or some enemy organization.

"So what do we do if we get some kind of clue from all this?" Pete whispered. "Who do we tell?"

"Depends on what we see or find out or just have to guess about," Harry said. "Heard anything from Stanzer? We might --"

He reached out and grabbed my arm as the image in the water blurred and swung around, off them, then back, then up at the sky, then followed some people walking past them.

What was going on?

The image blurred, and I was terrified we were going to lose the reception altogether. Then it steadied, and the view jumped back about ten feet. A man approached our folks through the crowd. He was hunched over, with a newspaper tucked under one arm, and a big cup of something pale gold and full of ice in the other hand. He was sort of square-built, and wore long pants, so he stood out from all the tourists. Shaggy blond hair, receding hairline, squashed sort of nose, and a scowl that implied nobody had any right to be as relaxed and happy as they looked. He stomped when everyone else strolled or meandered. Then he stopped short and kind of spread his legs a little like he needed steadier footing, and waited for our folks to meet up with him.

Part of me silently urged Mum and Pop to change their direction, even turn around and refuse to come near the guy. I knew that would have been a waste of breath if I could have spoken to them. They weren't the sort of people who ran away.

"I know him," Pete whispered.

"From where?" Harry said.

Pete just shrugged. I reached over and held his hand and we watched as the tourists sauntered past and our folks met up with the scowling man. They stayed back out of arm's reach, and out of reach of that newspaper, which he clutched in one hand and waved in Pop's face like he was going to poke him in the nose with it. The man did most of the talking, and I bristled a little, hating the way his lips twisted as he spat out his words. He was upset about something, and got more upset when Mum and Pop didn't seem to let him irritate or frighten them. Pop shook his head a few times, but didn't say much, other than what I was pretty sure was along the lines of "no," and other single-syllable words.

Without warning, the scowling man slapped the newspaper

flat at Mom. She reacted like anyone would, reaching up to block the expected blow, and clutched at the newspaper. The man let go and turned and stomped away. Our folks being the way they were, they didn't throw the newspaper away, not even with a handy trash can nearby. They opened up the newspaper.

Harry muttered something in Spanish, a long string I was pretty sure was cussing he never should have known when he was seven years old, before our folks adopted him. Whatever he said, I had to agree.

Inside the folded newspaper were photos. Mum and Pop flipped through a few of them. The photos were of us. Pete at school, working in the graphic arts class. Playing basketball in the high school gym. Working in the sound booth at church. Harry loading his truck at the printing plant in Valleyview, to bring papers up to the *Tattler* for delivery day. Me playing basketball with the Ezekiel's Wheels. And what was really frightening, the three of us sitting around the table in my kitchen. From that angle of the photo, there was no window for the camera to peer through. How did this guy get that particular camera angle without me knowing someone was there?

There were more photos, but Mum and Pop didn't look through many more. They exchanged a long look, then folded up the photos inside the newspaper again. Mum clutched the paper to her chest. Pop wrapped his arm a little tighter around her and they cut across the boardwalk pavement, between two shops, and headed up a long sandy pathway. A tall, wide building in pale pink rose up at the end of the path through palm trees. I had the feeling that was their hotel.

"How come there were more pictures of Pete than either of us?" Harry said.

"That's it. That's the guy," I blurted, and flinched when the light in the water flickered. The whole image sort of sloshed to the right, then to the left, and then suddenly the image and the light and the water were gone. I checked my watch. We had been watching Mum and Pop in Bermuda for nearly an hour.

"What guy?" Pete said.

"In England. When we came to get you, after your folks died. Put a flat brown hat on that guy's head. I'd swear he's the --"

"He's the guy who threw me off the balcony." His voice

cracked.

"You think he was looking for Pete, specifically?" Harry said.

I shook my head, thinking fast and feeling like I was stuck in neutral. I stopped the video part of my camera.

"He knew where I was already," Pete said. "All those pictures. He could have got to me any time he wanted."

"That's probably what he was proving to our folks," Harry said, nodding. "So, what did he want with our folks and why was he threatening them, showing them pictures of us? He was proving he could get close to us and nobody would ever know. The guy's desperate."

"So what happened to him when our folks vanished?" I said. "If he wanted something and they vanished, he might think they ran away. So why didn't he come after us, or at least break into our folks' place and look for whatever he wanted from them?"

"Maybe he got lost with them?" Pete looked a little pale in the moonlight. I couldn't be sure if he was scared or it was just the light.

"One way to find out." I waved my smartphone at them, by way of explanation. Then I looked around. It was chilly out here in the dark, among all this stone, with the quarry pools nearby. "Let's get home and figure out what we're going to tell the Colonel and Angela."

The boys had to help me stand, but I could take the couple of steps to my wheelchair. I gathered up the blankets while they were carrying the unused water to the Jeep and safely stowing the sealed containers. Then we got out of there.

Despite that little shock at the end, and the abrupt dying of the vision into the past, we were in a good mood. We had proved some of our theories. Tomorrow, we would start earlier in the evening, and we would have images taken from the video record to help us focus and pick up the story where it had left off. Little by little, an hour or two at a time -- in theory, at least -- we could follow our folks until we saw when and where and how they had vanished. Who was there. What had happened. Maybe some clue to how to bring them home.

Our good mood didn't last long. On the way home, Harry opened up my phone to start the playback. The camera caught nothing except the remarks we made and a hazy blob of light floating in the water, maybe a few hints of color. It took us a little more than half an hour to get from the quarries to my house, and in all that time, the image didn't improve. I had Harry turn off the playback. I wanted to tell him to erase the useless file, but I knew better. There was a chance Kurt might be able to coax something out of the blob of light, or somone at Hoax might have the technical wizardry to get what we needed. Not that I thought anyone would doubt us, if we told them everything we had seen and done that evening. I just wanted some proof.

Fortunately, Pete was a great sketch artist. And he had those vital images burned into his head. He drew half a dozen quick pencil sketches of Mum and Pop, along with some telling clues to where they had been on Bermuda. Then he drew the scowling man.

We stayed up until nearly 1am, discussing what we had seen and outlining what we had done, the time involved, when in the process something had changed. Then when we got up the next morning, we went over the report, to make sure everything was in place. I sent an abbreviated version of the report to Hayward. I wasn't going to tell him until we were face-to-face exactly where and how we had gotten the image of the scowling man.

I just told Hayward the truth: we had proof that a man on the island at the same time as our parents was the same man who had thrown Pete off the balcony of his parents' flat in England. The man had been caught coming out after ransacking the crates of the Crowder family's belongings. Whatever Hayward felt was necessary to be done with the drawing, which I scanned into the computer, that was up to him. I certainly wasn't going to try to tell him how to do his job.

That afternoon, after church, we picked up a picnic of sandwiches, potato salad, and utterly decadent brownies swirled with peanut butter and cream cheese, and took everything to Divine's Emporium. Then we reported everything to Angela. She inhaled softly and reached to catch hold of Pete's hand, when we got to the part about recognizing the scowling man. I was grateful she didn't scold us for conducting our experiment without asking permission or doing it without supervision. She didn't ask us any questions until we finished telling her everything, in the order that it happened.

"The question now," she said slowly, after looking through the sketches Pete had made, "is whether that man is a new enemy, if he focused on your parents because he's still trying to track something Jake and Emma found or learned before they died, or ..." She pursed her lips and flipped through the sketches one more time.

"Or?" Harry prompted.

"I honestly don't know," she said, finally looking up and meeting our eyes in turn. "That is the part that worries me. I sense there is another option, or perhaps several, but I can't seem to get it or them to step out of the fog so I can see them clearly enough. Ah, well, that is the penalty for growing old."

Pete snorted. That expressed quite eloquently what we were all probably thinking: Angela wasn't old and she would never get old. Angela saying she was getting old should have freaked us out a little bit. Especially me, since I had known her longer than the boys had. One of these days, I had the awful feeling I would look around and realize that I looked older than Angela -- and she had been an adult when I took my first trip to Divine's Emporium.

Angela chuckled and leaned over to kiss his cheek. Pete went bright red. To spare him, Harry took over the rest of the story, relating what we had done when we realized my camera didn't catch anything. How Pete had saved the day with his sketching ability. How we planned to trigger our next trip into the past using the last sketch of Mum and Pop.

"Why do you think we didn't pick up anything other than light?" Harry said. "There were hints of color and movement, but I watched the video twice from beginning to end, and there's still nothing. I've got some friends from school who could probably play with it and try to clear up the images, but I've got the feeling there won't be anything to clear up. Any idea why?"

"The simplest explanation?" Angela said after a few moments of frowning thought. "Most likely, there was nothing in the light. It was merely the vehicle or focal point. Whatever you saw ... it went directly to your minds, your souls. You saw, yes, but not with your physical eyes."

"How come that doesn't seem very safe?" Pete said. "Letting something kind of poke around in our heads and put movies in there?"

"Oh, it most likely isn't safe. But that isn't the same as being a threat." She patted his hand again. "Now, I hope you'll let me come with you next time. I want to see this fancy new trick you've learned for myself."

"We were hoping you'd come," I admitted. "Maybe we should invite the others? It isn't really right that we're doing this, especially if we can start using this to help people."

"No, not yet. Not large numbers. We must ease into this new tool granted us. Or perhaps it is a weapon. The important thing is to find out everything we can to try to bring Charlie and Rainbow home. Then we can risk what will happen when others are involved."

"You think there's a limit? Like we'll overload it and we won't be able to use it anymore?" Harry said.

"I hope not, but I've found it's often wise to proceed as if something is as fragile as a soap bubble and as dangerous as the Black Plague, and if something can go wrong, it will."

On that happy note, we headed out again. Angela left a note for Maurice, who had been spending the day with Jane and Kurt, visiting Hoax. They had taken several gallons of each kind of water, to experiment with. I was relieved to learn that they had done something without letting us know. That meant Kurt couldn't get angry with me for our experiment. Now the only one I had to worry about irritating was Felicity. She and Jake were spending the day with Troy and Diane at Put-in-Bay. I felt a little guilty that the need to report to Angela left Meggie all by herself, since Pete would have had her over to our house, or suggested the two of them doing something after church.

Yeah, being a guardian did mess with our personal lives, and the lives of our immediately family and closest friends.

We settled in the same place at the quarries, and filled the largest basin in the rock to overflowing, to get as much time as we could watching Mum and Pop. Either having twice as much water in the basin did it, or having another mind, or the fact that the extra mind was Angela, all the factors working together gave us three hours of viewing. Unfortunately, everything was in real time, with no fast forward controls. We followed Mum and Pop as they went back to their hotel suite and made phone calls and talked. Pop sketched, creating what looked like a map, while Mum did some internet searching. I couldn't remember seeing that map in the papers Hayward's people gave us. Had it been stolen or had our parents had that map with them when they vanished? I wrote a note to myself to check the search history of Mum's laptop. Maybe Athena or Wallace or Cosmo could track down the exact date and hour when different sites were searched?

The same antsy three-year-old was in control of where the lens went, following our parents. Fortunately, it didn't follow them into the bathroom, or when they stepped into the dressing room to change their clothes before they went out for lunch. It also didn't let us see much of what Mum was searching or enough of the map for Pete to reproduce it.

Scowling Man appeared across the street, watching from a seat on a fountain in the square where Mum and Pop had lunch in an outdoor café. Pop saw him and drew an arrow on a napkin, directing Mum to look. She used the old dropped knife gambit to bend down and look back while her head was down. When she sat up straight again, she wrinkled up her nose and crossed her eyes. Pop burst out laughing. I hoped that was a good sign.

"We should have brought something to eat with us," Harry remarked, when our folks finished their leisurely lunch and left the café.

"Next time, can we bring Kurt and maybe he can figure out how to put a fast forward switch on this thing?" Pete added.

As if speaking his name was a signal, my phone rang. Kurt. He and Jane and Maurice had just flown back from their trip to Hoax, and he wanted to know if we were still being Peeping Toms. I put him on speaker, and he did the same, so Maurice and Jane could hear what we had figured out and done. Funny, but Maurice's voice didn't come through the phone. Another aspect of the same magical conditions that didn't let us record the vision on my camera? Maurice wanted to try something. Kurt was up for it, and asked us to stay. Did we have enough water to do another viewing? Harry and Pete checked the jugs. Enough for another two-hour viewing time, if it all worked out the same. Angela asked Jane to go into her kitchen and pack some provisions for us.

We were all hungry. Maybe the effort of viewing drained us. As soon as Jane, Kurt and Maurice showed up, we chowed down while discussing what we had seen and done.

Kurt laughed when I explained my theory, and how we had proven it. He hadn't noticed the Halloween flyer on the bulletin board in the dorm.

"So between being out of phase with reality, and not being there in the phone booth, and not focusing on anything specific we wanted to see, no wonder we wasted all that time hanging out in the phone booth." He cocked an eyebrow at Jane. "So maybe we didn't need to dismantle the phone booth after all?"

"Oh, yeah, we did. With all that water dripping through, we had to do something." She shuddered, very clearly faking her disgust.

"So, Maurice, are you going to finally tell us what you're up to?" Angela said.

"I figure, if we can time travel, at least with our eyes, maybe we can solve a few mysteries. Especially if we've got some nasties trying to sneak into town, y'know?" Maurice fluttered down to land on Angela's ankle. She sat on the edge of a blanket with her legs extending out in front of her, with her ankles crossed.

"Can I just say this is kind of irritating?" Harry said, raising his hand halfway. "Remember, not all of us can see or hear the guy."

"How about this?" Maurice leaped up and dropped down hard on Harry's shoulder. My brother flinched and reached up, then seemed to catch on and didn't swipe away his new passenger. "Meggie and I figured this out." He stomped on Harry's shoulder, just off the seam. "Morse code."

"Problem," Pete said, when I explained. "We don't know Morse code."

"I suggest you learn, since Maurice has more than a year to go on his exile, and the more people he has to talk to, the less stressful my life is," Angela said. That earned a scowl from Maurice. A few seconds later she laughed, and he joined her.

"So what do you need to check out in the past?" Jane asked.

Maurice pointed at Pete. "I'm still chewing on that weirdness with that contract that burned up. I figure, either that thing was boobytrapped, or they realized you took it, and needed you to *not* see what you were about to agree to. So I figure … if we see what's in that contract, we get a better idea of who's gunning for you or your family or the whole town."

"Totally forgot about that," Pete said, when I told him what Maurice had said. "Think that was part of the curse or whatever that burned up the contract?" He snapped his fingers. "Hey, I took one of their pens. Maybe there's something weird about it."

"Where did you put it?" Angela said. "You haven't been using it, have you?"

"It's summer. What would I need to sign lately?"

"Good. Get it, bring it to me. The sooner the better. Just in case."

Pete and I were the only ones who had seen and touched the contract, so we set up on either side of the basin to focus. Harry and Kurt poured the water in, while we concentrated on remembering. Maurice hovered between us, waiting.

"What's that dark cloud?" Jane asked. She stood behind me.

"I don't see one," Pete said.

"That's all I see," Maurice said.

"What do you see?" Angela stood behind Pete and looked over him, down into the water.

"It's pretty hazy. Not bright. But ..." I concentrated and narrowed my eyes. "It's the Pi Surprise office. Kind of hazy, cloudy, which is weird because it was a bright, sunny day."

There was my Jeep, halfway into the thickening haze. I focused, trying to remember the sequence of events that day when we had gone to the lawn ornament company to sign Pete's contract.

A streak of light shot through the swirling, oily-looking haze that filled the building. It retreated to a tiny point, and that point moved out with two dark shapes that turned into me and Pete, coming out of the building kind of fast. I was digging in my backpack while Pete pushed my wheelchair. I pulled something out, and that spark flashed again.

I knew what that light was, what was in my hand.

My keychain. With the beads that Kerri was so interested in.

I felt kind of sick, wondering what would have happened to those beads, that light, if I had given Kerri the keychain to look at it.

Pop had taught me to listen to my gut instinct, even when it seemed unreasonable. Maybe especially when it seemed the most unreasonable. My gut instinct that day told me not to let my keychain out of my hand until I got home.

"Oh, that's not good," Maurice said.

"What isn't?" I looked down into the hazy image, where Pete and I were getting into my Jeep.

"You don't see them?" He bobbed lower, so low I thought his toes might dip into the surface of the water. "Do you see them?" he asked, tipping his head up to look at Angela.

She nodded, lips pressed flat, a few tiny lines forming around her eyes. Her hands rested on Pete's shoulders now, giving me a distinct impression of being protective.

Kerri came running out of the building to confront us. I wondered if she was so distracted by the beads she wanted to get her hands on, she didn't notice we had taken the contract.

"What?" I had to ask, although that squirmy sensation in my gut told me I really didn't want to know.

"They're just … cloaked." Maurice shook his head and bobbed down far enough he had to stretch out, lying horizontal to the water's surface now. "Anything that puts that much effort into cloaking itself --"

"It, not them?" Jane asked.

"Believe it or not, the Fae don't know everything about interdimensional creepies and crawlies." He tried for a smirk. I appreciated the effort to lighten the mood, but he failed miserably, and it just made him look a little sick. "Anyway, what I was saying, anything that puts that much effort, that much energy into cloaking itself, so that even looking backward through time we can't make out anything but the cloak … and the fact you guys don't see them now, and didn't see them then … Angela told me about some of the nasty stuff you've been putting up with for years from the Rivals. These new enemies might make you wish the Rivals would come back, just for some comedy relief."

"Oh, great, just what we needed," Kurt muttered. I looked back and up at him, since he and Jane were standing pretty much behind me. He put his arm around her.

Then I looked at Angela, and for just a second, I flashed back to that whole bizarre incident my freshman year, and the psycho-social experiment and the energy building up on my dorm floor. And especially the way something had tried to take a bite out of Angela and drain her. I shivered, remembering how she had changed, just for a few moments, so sad and tired and old underneath it all. The way she talked about someone she had known, and wasn't even sure she had known him other than as a dream or a vision of what was to come.

"It's not a new enemy, is it?" I said, and it worried me that my words seemed to startle Angela, just a little, so she flinched and her eyes widened and she stared into my eyes for a heartbeat or two.

Then her usual smirk came back, and the color returned to her cheeks, although not all the way. She shook her head and said quietly, "No, I do not think this is a new enemy at all. For all we know, this is the power behind the Rivals. Behind the nastiness that has motivated the Grandstones all these generations. The creeping sense of something standing just outside the pool of light that Neighborlee creates in the darkness." She wrapped her arms around herself and gave a little shudder, while a sharp kind of amusement danced in her eyes. "It stands outside the light and hates it, and doesn't realize that its anger and hatred cripples its reasoning, and drains its power. It stands alone, even though it might have enormous numbers. It is constantly hungry, even as it drains the protective energy generated by our town. Because we are not alone, we are united, we stand for each other. And we have been granted an insight into its actions. We have been warned."

She gestured down at the image in the basin of water, where Pete and I were in my Jeep, coming up the main drag through town. "Thank you for remembering, and being irritated, Maurice. We would have lost a weapon in our battle."

"Does someone want to explain the parts we've been missing?" Harry said.

I choked on half-laughter and half-embarrassment. My brothers were so much a part of everything we were doing, sometimes it was hard to remember there were some things they couldn't see or hear, like Maurice and the winkies, and the sense of energy vibrating through things. Angela filled them in on what Maurice had been saying.

"Focus," Maurice said. "Latch your eyeballs onto that contract and focus really hard." He pointed at the image of my Jeep. The lens or whatever it was that guided what we saw now swung around, so we were looking into the passenger window of my Jeep. Pete was unfolding the contract and looking through it again. "Focus harder. Man, can't you magnify or -- okay, that works."

Chapter Eleven

I bit my lip to keep from saying that I hadn't done anything. Maybe just wanting to see closer changed things? Like a zoom lens moving in, the image slipped through the open window and seemed to perch on Pete's shoulder while he flipped through the contract for the fourth or fifth time.

"Is it just me, or is that nothing like the English alphabet?" Kurt said.

"It is not you," Angela said, her voice thin and quiet, sharp like a knife, and I shuddered with gratitude that she had never used that tone on me or anyone I knew.

"That's kind of freaky," Pete muttered, as the words on the page shifted, like one of those special effects in a movie where words on a computer screen rearranged themselves, changing from one language and alphabet to another. For instance, changing from elf writing to English. This time it was more like changing from an alien alphabet that looked pretty ugly, to the English alphabet. "Why's it doing that?"

"Pull back, away from the -- there." Angela pointed, as the zoom lens pulled away and my Jeep grew smaller, and we saw writhing, dark shapes following us down the road as we made the first turn into the residential section, to go to Divine's.

They were on the far side of the road, and stayed there, churning, as my Jeep went down the side street. It was hard to tell their numbers, but several of them in a clump crossed the road, leaving more than half of them behind. The ones that followed my Jeep sort of disintegrated and faded with every driveway they passed. They were half the length of the street behind my Jeep when I made the next turn, right, onto the long street where Divine's sat at the far end. The second my Jeep turned onto the street, there was something like a flash, like I had driven through a wall of light. The shadowy remains of the dark, churning things seemed to turn somersaults as they reversed direction in midair. The flash that wasn't really light, wasn't color, more a sense of brightness, hit those shadowy things. It was like they turned to powder and blew away. I looked up in time to see Angela's thin smile and her single, short nod, satisfaction, maybe relief.

Okay, that made sense. It sort of backed up some theories I had had since I was a child, that the closer I got to Divine's, the safer I would be. There were layers of protection in Neighborlee. It wasn't just one shield protecting and enclosing the whole town, but different layers. Maybe the closer they were to Divine's, the stronger they were, maybe with that sort of early warning system built into them, that made it possible for Angela to know when something or someone was coming.

I put my theories aside for later, to think about them and clarify, and bring up for discussion with Angela when things settled down. If things ever settled down.

We were all quiet as we watched my Jeep in the watery vision, pulling up to the front gate of Divine's. Pete got out. I settled into my chair. We approached the gate. In another moment, the contract would self-destruct.

No, wait ... part of the contract had *vanished*, and part of it had turned to black char and then evaporated.

"Banzai!" Maurice hollered, and dove into the water.

Instead of a splash, there was a sizzling sound and I swear I saw smoke rise off his wings.

"Maurice!" Angela cried, as close to a shriek as I had ever heard come out of her throat.

She was scared, and that just scared me.

"What'd he do?" Pete shouted, nearly in chorus with Harry.

"No!" Jane called, and reached for Maurice.

Her hands bounced off the dome of light from the vision.

Okay, so that proved Maurice's theory about being in different time streams.

Maurice let out a roar that I just did not think was possible, considering how tiny his vocal cords were. He arched upward, hauling part of that demonic contract with him. Out of the light. Trailing more smoke. Really rancid-smelling smoke, like something had rotted to the edge of liquification before it was set on fire with kerosene.

In the vision, part of the contract vanished, and the rest of it did what we had seen it do the first time around.

"Taa daa!" Maurice said. Or at least he tried to. His voice sort of cracked, ending on a whimper, and he tossed the piece of contract to Angela. Then he landed on my knee. I wanted to cuddle him, but I could see this shimmering smoke rising off him, like he was still on fire, or ready to burst into flames, and I was afraid of hurting him.

Yeah, and I was afraid of scorching my fingers.

Angela flinched, and I knew for just a second, she was afraid of touching that dratted thing. She twisted her sleeve around to insulate her fingers and snatched that piece of paper, singed all around the edges.

"Ma -- aa -- an!" Kurt groaned. "Are you suicidal or have you been mainlining the cherry cola?" He grinned and scooped up Maurice and cradled him. His hand shook. Jane snatched up the bottle of neutralizer and sprinkled it on him. Yeah, there was sort of a moment of sizzle, and that scorched smell vanished and Maurice's wings kind of went droopy. He grinned like he was loopy and closed his eyes and turned his face up to the drops. Jane kept sprinkling until he was soaked.

Right about then, getting sloshed on diet cherry cola sounded like a really good idea. I kind of envied the weird bio-chemistry of the Fae, that diet cherry cola got them silly, but they were able to shake off the effects with just willpower. No hangovers, no loss of control like alcohol did to Humans.

Yeah, and I kind of envied how the Fae used dark chocolate like a tonic and cure-all. Any excuse to eat dark chocolate.

Which Maurice definitely needed. Fortunately, I always carried some chocolate and fruit leather, to deal with emergencies. Whenever I did use my mutant or alien or whatever abilities, it usually meant over-using them, straining myself into a headache. Sometimes nosebleeds.

All the above happened in the space of about ten seconds, a whole lot less time to play out than it took to narrate the sequence of events. It took longer to get my emergency supplies out of the backpack hanging off my chair, and break off a square of Special Dark and hold it out to Maurice.

"Marry me," he groaned, and took it in both hands.

The vision shimmered for about two seconds, then there was the sensation of a silent *pop*, and the bowl in the rock was empty and dry.

Angela studied the piece of contract. For about five seconds. The fragment sparkled, if something that was darkening from the torn edge down to where she held it with her sleeve could sparkle. Then it turned to dust, and that dust vanished before it fell apart, out of the form of the sheet of paper.

"Did you read any of it?" Maurice said, through a mouthful of chocolate.

"Enough to have a good idea of the nasty mischief those people were hoping to implement." She shuddered. "Maurice, I appreciate the risk you took …" She sighed.

"Not worth it?" He shrugged, then took another huge bite of chocolate and chewed vigorously. "Don't know if I proved my theory or proved it won't work."

"What were you trying to prove?" Harry asked, when I repeated Maurice's side of the conversation.

Was this what it felt like for translators at the United Nations?

"Being immune, since I'm from a different time stream."

"Yes, but you've been living here more than seven months, and you were inside the shop when the contract originally self-destructed," Jane pointed out.

"But he did reach through the water or whatever the water became, when it provided a viewing portal into the past," Angela said, spacing her words out as if she wasn't quite sure of them. "So there is something … advantageous? Something beneficial for us in Maurice, or perhaps any Fae, when it comes to dealing with the time differential." She shook her head, and her gaze went distant. "This is something to think about for a while before any further experimentation."

"My aching wings thank you." Maurice saluted her by raising the last handful of chocolate, then shoved it into his mouth.

"Okay, all of that is interesting," Kurt said. "Agreed. Put the time-traveling ability of Fae aside for a while. What else did we learn today, besides that we do sort of have some focus controls?"

"That contract was an attempt to create a corridor, a safe passageway into Neighborlee," Angela said. "The words were an ancient, powerful language. Essentially, Pete would have been agreeing to full cooperation, no questions asked, giving them access to his home, the things he saw and did. His very thoughts."

"Like signing away his soul?" Kurt muttered.

"Not like," Maurice snarled. "I didn't catch all of it, but there were pieces that certainly looked like the kid would be agreeing to give them all his energy, all his potential, basically emptying himself out and letting them use him like a whaddayacallit thingy in that movie we were watching the other day. You know, like sending in robots to check out alien worlds."

"A probe," I said.

"It was a contract of full and utter and unbreakable subjugation," Angela said. "And because Pete is such an established part of this community, he would have brought those malevolent creatures everywhere he went, and they would have been welcome, because they were part of him."

"Nuh uh," Pete said. He tried to smile, but I could see how he fought something that was part anger and part sickness and part terror. He struggled to his feet. "We talked about this stuff in that crazy couple of months when we were studying cults and demon possession and stuff in youth group. They can't take my soul, because I gave it to Jesus. He ain't giving it back."

"Very true," Angela said, and squeezed his shoulders. "However, you would have given those creatures access to the deepest, most essential part of you. They would have used you as a conduit to invade Neighborlee. To invade Divine's."

"This isn't the Rivals, is it?" I said, trying not to sound as sick as I felt. Pete was my little brother. Someone was trying to chew on his soul, even if they couldn't swallow.

"This is way out of their league," Jane said. "They don't work with magic. Basically, they see themselves as scientists, smarter than everybody, granting themselves a superiority that gives them the right to rule the Human race. What Angela is talking about … I'm scared, and I wouldn't be surprised if a lot of people at the Sanctum are scared by this too."

"That shows wisdom," Angela murmured.

"There's wisdom, and there's being a wise guy," Harry said. "You know, you're forgetting something. I agree it's pretty rotten, tricking Pete into slavery and brainwashing him and all that comes with it, just signing a contract like that. Pretty nasty magic. But I don't think he was the target. He was just the gate."

"To get at Divine's, right," Kurt said.

"No … they were using Pete to get at me," I said, and I was

really glad I was still sitting on the ground, because the sensation of the world sort of jerking sideways was so strong, I might have fallen out of my chair. "They wanted *me* to sign Pete's contract, as his legal guardian. I bet that fancy wording included me in everything they were going to wrap around Pete."

"Undoubtedly," Angela said, nodding. "While Pete would have given them a doorway, including you, a guardian, someone who shed blood to protect this town ... the potential damage is incalculable."

"So how do we get these guys? We gotta strike back. Anybody else getting kind of sick of just being on the defensive all the time?" Kurt said, his voice sharp and rough.

Yeah, he was my big brother again. Kind of nice.

"Oh, we, or rather Lanie and Pete, already struck them hard. They lost some of their army, when they followed Lanie and Pete, most likely trying to get the contract back. They lost their power the moment Pete got that contract out of their possession. They revealed their hand and their latest plan the moment Pete and Lanie refused to cooperate, refused to trust and take them at their word. Every time someone resists their schemes and sees through their lies and doubts them, they lose power, because so much of what they are is tied up in deception and destruction." Angela spread her arms, hands palms up, taking in all of us. "We are united, with one focus and purpose. We stand in the light, we sacrifice ourselves for the good of others. We stand for life and healing. All they want to do is devour and envelope everything in darkness, and even as they are forced to work together, they are alone, forever trying to subjugate each other. We have already dealt them a terrible blow, simply by resisting. No need to attack."

"Besides," Jane said, "where would we aim when we do attack? Do you know where they are? It makes sense to me that we sit back and prepare, stay alert, and let them come to us. Let them waste their energy coming to us, and like in karate, use their energy and momentum against them."

Kurt scowled at her, but I was relieved to see it was a teasing kind of scowl. Maybe he felt a little foolish, but he didn't really mind. Yeah, that was love at work. She was good for him. And if he wasn't good for her, I'd get to work on him.

~~~~~
~~~~~

Stanzer called to report on contacting the injured girl. I think he just needed to talk, to help him work out his impressions and come up with a plan. He had met up with her in the dreamplain. She was confused and slowly regaining her memories. Their contact was hazy, little more than an awareness of her presence, and to know she was aware of him.

He had found the nursing home where they were keeping her. It was on the edge of the city park, with an exercise course and jogging trail. He had already had several close calls with park rangers discovering his hiding place. The number of park rangers on patrol had doubled, and he had located all the guards on patrol around the nursing home. Then that morning, he had seen the girl climb out a window of an upper level, jump down several levels, from one flat rooftop to another in the facility, and sneak past the guards. He didn't know whether to be amused, to admire her, or curse her for putting herself at risk. There was no way she could get very far before her guards came running after her. He had stayed in his hiding place in the park and watched her come closer. For all he knew, she had sensed him and was coming looking.

From only a few hundred yards away, he had watched her rest on the edge of the jogging trail. She had a bandage wrapped around her head, and smaller bandages wrapped around her arms. She looked pale and thin, like she had only just gotten back on her feet. Stanzer said he had waited and prayed and begged the Hounds to show up and approach her, and lead her to him, because he didn't dare get any closer.

Before he got any response to his prayers, or before he even got his plan solidified in his head, a man and a woman came down the jogging path. Stanzer wasn't close enough to hear them, or see enough details, but it seemed like they were harassing the girl from the moment they met up with her. Then suddenly the man pulled a knife on her. The girl spun and kicked and defended herself. Before Stanzer could take more than a few running steps out of hiding, a park ranger pulled up and broke up the fight, and at gunpoint took the three of them away. Suddenly government agents were swarming the park and all the land surrounding the old nursing home. Stanzer had to run and find another hiding place. He watched all day, but the girl wasn't brought back. Now he had to start from scratch, tracking her down again.

I offered to come up to help. It might be a nice break for all of us, to get away from town and focus on someone else's problems for a change. Stanzer thanked me, but there was nothing he could do while London searched government communication channels.

It wasn't like I *wanted* to step foot outside of Neighborlee for a while. Something nastier than the Rivals was gearing up to attack us. Big Ugly had been quiet for a long time now. Maybe we had grown complacent, maybe we had hoped that he had given up, or just fallen asleep deeper and longer than after previous attacks. The battle wasn't over by a long shot.

We met with Ford and the Sheridans to discuss our new discoveries. We set up a schedule of spending a few hours at a time, filling the basin in the rock and watching Mum and Pop do the touristy researcher thing. We really didn't have much control, so it wasn't like we could press a fast forward button and get to the interesting parts. We had to sit through everything in real time. We calculated just a few days passed between Mum and Pop making the video to send to us and when they vanished. We couldn't sit around the clock at the quarries, watching the vision in the water, so it would take a lot longer than real time. Anticipating how long we had to wait to find out what had happened, where our folks were, and what they had been doing when they disappeared ... it felt like that would take forever. On the plus side, this was going to take maybe a week, compared to nearly two years of waiting already. So why was I complaining?

Hey, I was an education major, not a psych major. Don't ask me how the Human brain supposedly works.

Then we caught a break. A big one.

London and Sherwood found video clips and police photos and files posted online, and located Scowling Man. They were still there in the electronic files because *he* was still there, an ongoing mystery, in Bermuda.

In a hospital. He had been found unconscious in a little park-like area, with a monument to some local historical event and person. No one was sure how long he had been there because there had been no ruckus, no strange lights or sounds or smells. He was just tucked into a shadowy corner, limp, unresponsive, and carrying no identification whatsoever. No wallet, no personal belongings, no hotel key. Maybe someone had mugged him and cleaned him out before dumping his body?

Considering this was Scowling Man, and he had been found the morning *after* my parents had officially vanished from Bermuda, we were betting he hadn't been mugged. Maybe someone had found him wherever he had collapsed and robbed him, and then hid him so he wouldn't be discovered right away.

He was still unidentified. Every once in a while, he would regain consciousness and be able to speak a little bit. Usually, he would try to get out of his hospital bed and walk away, and even get angry and uncooperative. He never answered questions, but asked a lot of questions. Mostly along the lines of where he was, where "they" were, what "they" had done to him. He never said who "they" were, never gave names, and never explained what he thought had happened to him. He also refused to admit who he was. Before any pressure could be put on him to get answers, he lost consciousness again, or lost lucidity.

No one had reported him missing. The cruise lines and airlines didn't have anyone matching his description in their manifest. More important, they didn't have any missing customers or report any passengers missing a departure. The only clue to his origins was that when he did speak, he had a Midwestern accent.

His accent made it easier for Col. Hayward to act, once London gave him all the information. He flew down to Bermuda to personally take charge of Scowling Man. After all, if he was a resident of the United States, then his country of origin had a responsibility to take care of him. The Sheridan group had the personnel and facilities to take a semi-unconscious prisoner and safely tuck him away where he could be tended by Gifted healers, and hopefully, eventually, get some answers out of him.

One interesting theory that we hoped was a point in our favor: Scowling Man couldn't have been in Bermuda hassling my parents on someone's orders. Otherwise, they should have retrieved him when he ended up in the hospital. If his bosses weren't waiting for a report, then maybe he was freelancing.

On the other hand, maybe we were dealing with really nasty folks who just abandoned any tool or minion that failed or disappointed them. Maybe that would work in our favor, when Scowling Man woke up and stayed awake. If he ever did. There was no telling for a while.

We settled into our shifts of teams watching in the water. It took us nearly three days of watching to complete a full day of Mum and Pop's activities. We couldn't stay in that part of the quarries at night. The rangers on patrol would politely ask us to leave, or just plain ask the wrong questions. Having people camped out from sunrise to sunset would also attract too much of the wrong kind of attention. So we had to break up the sessions. It was kind of interesting, and knowing my folks, never boring. We watched them visiting little historic sites on the island, visiting government records offices, talking with wrinkled up, elderly men and women who looked like they were more than a hundred years old.

I really wished one of us knew how to read lips. Sometimes we got glimpses of the notes they took, or the names of files or the wording in some of the documents they looked at or copied. Some of the material was among the files and personal items retrieved from their hotel room. A lot of it wasn't. So what were our parents doing with that material the day they vanished?

An interesting side note: A few times as we followed Mum and Pop around the island, we glimpsed Arthur Sheridan. He definitely didn't look like a tourist, always walking from one place to another with a determined stride. He wasn't wearing a suit coat or tie, but he had a briefcase. Talk about making himself stand out in a crowd. I was there twice watching the pool at the same time Arthur was there on viewing duty, and both times we caught glimpses of him. He just shook his head.

"No fool like an old fool," he said the first time. "I couldn't have done anything more effective at drawing attention to myself. And to top it all off, I was oblivious to the picture I made."

"What were you there on the island for?" I had to ask. He hadn't said before this, not in clear enough detail to satisfy me. Yes, he was a valuable ally, someone I liked a lot, someone I trusted. If he said his reasons for being on the island had nothing to do with my folks or their research, then I believed him. Still, a lot of little things were getting irritating, just because of our lack of progress. The not knowing was one of those little irritating details.

"Following up on clues, mysterious bits of information, and someone who was trying to make contact but hiding their origination point." He frowned, watching himself walk across the plaza in the background, while my folks were having fun bartering with a spice vendor in the open air market in the foreground. "At the time, we thought they were afraid. Now ..." He shrugged.

"You think maybe it was a trap?"

"Maybe someone was using our timid friend to draw me into a trap, or maybe it was just a test. Who knows? When I woke up, I was in the hospital, my hotel room had been ransacked, and I still have a hole in my memory, for several days before the attack. We don't even know if I was physically attacked by someone, or I suffered some kind of seizure or fit. I went down a flight of steps in a remote location, and wasn't found for hours. If the damage was done before or during the fall, we have no way of knowing."

"Maybe you were close enough to my folks when whatever hit them, hit them ... that was collateral damage?" I offered.

"Maybe."

That little talk got him thinking. And we discovered that watching through the pool and seeing himself moving about different locations in Bermuda triggered some memories. Arthur showed up at all the viewing sessions after that, hoping to see himself and get more of his memories back.

The theorized date our parents vanished was getting closer in the timeline. We grew impatient with sitting out in the sun, on bare rock at the old quarries, just watching them wander around the island. Part of me wanted to shout, "Just get on with it!" but that was a stupid idea. Not just because my folks couldn't have heard me, but more because even though I wanted answers, I really didn't want to *see* what made them vanish. Kind of like that point in reading a book or watching a movie, where I just knew the heroine was going to do something totally stupid and I cringed for her. For all we knew, a rift through space and time opened up and swallowed them, without any warning, with no clues, meaning we wouldn't be able to figure out how to bring them back. Or worse, we would see our parents gunned down by island crooks, who then threw their bodies into the ocean.

Then Stanzer returned to Neighborlee, and his story was a welcome, brief distraction. I had a little bit of a guilt trip for wallowing in my own pity party. His problems did a good job slapping me back into balance.

"She's Dandova," he told us, when we had all gathered at Divine's.

He paused, giving us time to digest that bit of news. We needed time, because the girl who had called down the blue lightning when the criminal mastermind, Archby, killed her friends, was only sixteen years old. Dandova was only four years younger than Stanzer, so she should be twenty-four. What happened to those eight years?

Even more important: Dandova wasn't with Stanzer now. That was probably a bigger story and problem than the shift in her age.

We were all gathered outside in Angela's garden, some of us sitting on the ground, Angela and Ford on the swing. It was a gorgeous August day.

"Now I understand why we couldn't find any blue storms to indicate where the other members of the Hunt landed when the Hounds brought us to Earth," Stanzer continued. "We've been separated in *time and distance.* We all left pretty much at the same time, when Gahlmorag invaded and struck at all our clan house towers. But we arrived on Earth at *different* times. I've been here fourteen years, but Dandova has only been here six."

"Ouch," Athena murmured.

"I promised her I'd find her, when we got wherever the Hounds sent us, and we'd be together. But I didn't find her, and she's been alone and ..." He groaned and finally stopped pacing in front of the swing. Rubbing at his face, like a very tired little boy, he folded up and sat down hard. I felt the thud of his landing.

"I pushed her too hard. I guess being alone so long bothered me a lot more than I thought. We argued a few times, and then ... yeah, there were all those government people to get through, and the mess from catching Archby. Catching him in the act is the important thing and Dandova did it. Not the Feds, not the big tough-guy private eye." He jabbed himself in the breastbone with his thumb. "A smart-mouth, daredevil sixteen-year-old, who ended up taking a big chance to protect me, after Archby poisoned me."

"Whoa, whoa," Harry broke in. "Stop shoveling the guilt and just tell us what happened, as it happened, okay? You're leaving out all the good stuff."

Chapter Twelve

Angela chuckled softly, and that sent a bright flush across Stanzer's face. At the same time, he seemed to relax a little. He really was worn out.

He had managed to find the new safe house where the Feds had moved Dandova -- Dawn, he corrected himself. She thought of herself as Dawn Dover. That was the name the authorities gave her when she was found and given to the child welfare system. By this time, he had made enough contact with her in the dreamplain, he theorized the injured girl was a member of the Hunt who had been too young to remember anything when she came to Earth. He believed for a short time that his Dandova was an agent, who caught up with the teens while Archby's men were murdering them, realized one was a member of the Hunt, and called down blue lightning to defend her. Working on the theory that Dandova was protecting the girl who was the only witness against Archby, he approached the safe house and let himself get caught. He wanted to confront the adult Dandova.

Dawn overheard some of the confrontation when Stanzer was taken prisoner. By this time, she had remembered enough of her heritage as a member of the Hunt to call a Hound to her. She went invisible and moved through the house to the pantry where Stanzer had been locked up. With the help of the Hound, Stanzer walked through a wall and they escaped the house, walking far enough away for a conversation in safety. Finding out she was sixteen, not twenty-four, and the seriousness of her situation, knocked Stanzer off balance. He was willing to let the agents keep protecting Dawn until he could figure out what to do next.

Sherwood made contact with him about then and provided more information on Archby. His pattern was to keep digging and striking until he got what he wanted. In this case, that information the murdered agent had stolen from him. Stanzer settled down to watch the house, to try to spot the first attempt to get at Dawn. A Hound helped him investigate the safe house and find all the weak places in the security.

So did the enemy. Stanzer had sent a note to Dawn with a Hound, warning her when Archby's men found the secret escape tunnel leading to the safe house. Dawn and a woman agent escaped, but the woman was injured. Stanzer helped her, then he and Dawn took off. They decided the best way to end the threat from Archby was to lead him into a trap. Stanzer had taken a phone from one of the attackers, so he called Archby and offered him the information his men had killed for. Then he and Dawn went to Cedar Point, to lead Archby and his men on a wild goose chase, lost in the crowds at the amusement park, and set them up for the Feds to catch them.

In the end, Stanzer's plan worked, but Archby managed to poison him with room service food. With him incapacitated, Dawn went out to face Archby and his men as bait. The Feds saved the day, but Stanzer was so infuriated with her and his own mistakes, they argued. He knew the name of the orphanage where she was living, but he had no idea how he was going to make things right.

"We belong together. I promised her I wouldn't push her, and I'd wait until she was old enough, and she was willing and ..." He shrugged. "Do you have any idea how it feels, to find someone who remembers the people and the places you do, and she's everything you ever hoped for? But she's too young, and you feel like a dirty old man every time you want to just hold her, forget about ... I have that whole building, just waiting for the day I find the rest of the Hunt, and I can't bring her home."

"No," Angela said slowly. "You can't. Not yet. There's work that needs to be done. Official, legal permission. Guardianship. Arranging to transfer all her school records, and of course we need to work quickly, to get her up here and settled in before school starts." She laughed at Stanzer, who stared at her, his mouth falling a little farther open with every sentence. "John, of course we're going to help you bring her home. Of course you two need to be together. You're going to be absolutely useless if she isn't here where you can check up on her. And some of the things you left unsaid, I can guess. You're going to eat yourself alive with jealousy, thinking of her in school with all those high school boys who are such idiots nine-tenths of the time when it comes to smart, brave, independent girls."

"Even if we get the right permissions and authorizations, I can't make her come up here," he said, after visibly sorting through different responses. Stanzer looked sort of pitiful with gratitude and hope, and those hopes visibly shattering a few seconds later. "She's pretty furious with me."

"Ask her. Apologize. I can't say I know how she's feeling, but I've been close to the same situation," Jane said. "I can guess. Going to Hoax was the scariest thing that ever happened to me, once I started figuring out my Gift. But when I realized I was surrounded by people who understood, who knew the rules, yeah, I knew I belonged. Bring Dawn up here. She'll become part of the family fast enough, even if she's still mad at you, she'll get over it."

"Yeah," I said. "Family. All us freaks gotta stick together."

"Speak for yourself," Pete said. Which just made all of us laugh.

~~~~~

Scowling Man had a short period of lucidity right after Hayward got him transferred from Bermuda and put into the custody of the private little clinic run by Sheridan allies. Enough lucidity to react to his changed surroundings and have a panic attack. I didn't see him. I didn't want to see him, because I was convinced he was involved in whatever made my folks disappear. The very attentive, helpful people in the clinic calmed him down and convinced him he was not only back in the United States, but he was safe from "them." Whoever "them" might have been. They convinced him they were protecting him, and his enemies couldn't find him.

Two options. Either he thought my parents had zapped him, or he was working for someone and got caught in the backwash of whatever his evil bosses did to my folks. Or maybe he was just terrified of whatever punishment his evil bosses would levy on him for failing his mission. Whatever it was.

The healers got a few answers out of him. His name was Carl Tucker, age fifty-two. They weren't sure if he was fifty-two when he ran into my folks in Bermuda, or if he was aware of the passage of time and that was his age now. He was a private investigator. He either wouldn't say or couldn't remember what he was investigating in Bermuda. Daniel was back in town and he came to the office to bring me the report and catch up on what we had been doing, experimenting with the water.

"There's more to this than Tucker just being there and getting
~~~~~

zapped about the same time your parents vanished," he said. "Maybe the same thing got my grandfather, but Tucker was turned into coma man because he was physically closer to ground zero. What's special about this guy?"

"Nothing. Yet. We're still not sure if he was working for anyone, or he was trailing my folks for his own reasons. Maybe he thinks they have something that he was looking for about ten years ago. For all I know, he's involved in Pete's parents getting killed."

"Whoa -- wait a second. Pete's ... okay, blame jet lag." Daniel grinned and settled back in Franny's desk, which always seemed to be unoccupied when he came to check on me at the office. "I knew all three of you were adopted, but I forgot that fun little detail. Pete's parents were killed?"

"Yeah, they were friends of my folks, investigative writers, following a treasure hunt, basically. There was something a little weird about the whole accident, while they were investigating an archeological site. The Colonel is Pete's only living relative. He couldn't claim Pete, to protect him from people who are just extremely nasty enough to punish a little six-year-old for crimes his grandparents committed."

"Okay, that just sent a shiver down my back." He leaned forward. "So you stepped in?"

"Harry and I got totally new identities and histories and flew to England. Mum and Pop were out of the country, working on a book. We took custody of Pete at the hotel where the child welfare people were keeping him. Despite everyone telling us to just let them take care of the packing and get out of the country, we went back to the little town where his parents had lived, to get some things he wanted. We met up with their wonderful landlady, and this Tucker bozo came out of the flat just when we got there."

I flinched, remembering what came next, and reached for my big sipper bottle of lemonade. My throat got dry just thinking of Pete sailing through the air, out over the river, even though I knew he survived without a scratch. A long, messy, sloppy skid through a muddy cow pasture, yes. Scratches or worse, no. It helped to have a big sister who could kinda-sorta fly.

"What happened?" Daniel asked, his voice soft. There was sympathy in his big dark eyes, like he knew something awful had nearly struck us.

"The big jerk grabbed Pete, who was only six, this firecracker, constantly on the move. He grabbed Pete, and we were on a balcony on the third floor, looking out over the river. And he threw Pete off the balcony."

"He landed in the river and was okay, right?"

"I didn't even think. I just jumped and swooped out and caught him and kept going. Across a river ten yards wide. You should have heard all the people in this funky little English town, coming up with all sorts of weird reasons why it was perfectly logical for us landing so far on the other side. In a huge, muddy cow pasture. Emphasis on cow patties."

Daniel grimaced, and I thought his throat worked like he fought not to be sick. Suddenly, I could breathe again and the fury-horror from that long ago afternoon didn't ache through me anymore.

"So why did he say he threw Pete?"

"He didn't. He got away in all the fuss. I thought he just threw Pete for a distraction, but now seeing him trailing my folks in the water visions, I have to wonder. What was he after that day? Did he deliberately try to kill Pete for some reason? When I see him tailing my folks, and then running into them and Pop getting so coldly angry ..." I shuddered. "I want to blame him for what happened to them."

"He's affected by something otherworldly," Daniel said, looking down at his clasped hands instead of me. I had grown to know many of his ticks and mannerisms. This told me he knew something he didn't want to tell me, but he would because he thought it was his duty. "My mother and grandmother both have looked him over. They brought in some of our specialists. Touch healers, who get into the spirit to heal. Tucker is only half of himself. Physically. Which is affecting his mind. It's why he sleeps so much."

"Wait a second. What do you mean by half of himself?" I flinched, remembering too late we were in the newspaper office and we weren't alone.

Even if there was no one in sight in the editorial "house" of the long row of connected stores that had been turned into one building, someone could have heard us. As much as I really enjoyed being able to talk about the ordinary weirdness of my life with someone who understood, it didn't pay to get careless. Despite the protective field that touched the minds of the people of Neighborlee, pushing the limits of just how much weirdness the "ordinary" folk of our town could handle was just plain reckless.

"He's not entirely there. It's like half his substance is missing." Daniel shrugged. "Hey, don't ask me. I'm just passing on what the healers are theorizing."

"Doesn't help much."

"I don't know. It kind of feels like a jumping off point for finding answers. Or at least ideas for answers."

"Yeah," I had to agree. "It kind of does."

The next time it was my turn to watch over the basin of water, Scowling Man, aka Carson Tucker, popped out of the crowd, regular as clockwork, and followed my folks. He didn't really seem to be trying to stay unseen. For all I could tell, he wanted them to see him. Maybe he was trying to irritate Pop into getting into an argument or making mistakes.

Harry and I had the early morning shift, but the scene playing out before us was late afternoon. I was getting a little jealous of the exotic locations Mum and Pop got to enjoy, even as they put in a lot of leg work and probably wasted time to irritate Tucker. Of course, there was no sound, so we couldn't really tell what they learned when they interviewed people.

Nothing really happened, except it was nice seeing Mum and Pop being themselves, getting stares and then defrosting nearly everyone they ran into. Nearly everyone. Some people were just stick-in-the-muds, or to be honest, sticks in certain portions of their anatomy. They seemed to get insulted with the cheerful Yanks who looked so weird, more weird than a lot of the tourists swarming their lovely island. Still, our folks were having a good time and trying to spread their good spirits to everyone they encountered.

My phone rang at about the end of the second hour of watch duty. It was Daniel. He wanted me to know that Tucker had awakened and was, if not lucid, then at least talking and reacting to something. He was terrified, trying to run away before the fog got him and ate him, just like it ate "them." Whoever "them" was. (I was saying that a little too much lately.)

"Funny thing is," he continued, "it's been happening regular as clockwork since Gram got him settled at the clinic. My grandfather made the connection." He chuckled. "It's like a game with him, kind of like a rivalry thing. He's still kind of seething, and laughing about it, how he missed all the clues so many years ago, and was working against Hoax and the people who stayed in town. So anyway ... I gave him the update on what you were doing with the water experiment, and he had the two reports sitting on his desk, right next to each other and ..." He sighed. "You're watching the water view right now, aren't you?"

"Yes ..." I shivered a little and Harry gave me one of those "so are you going to fill me in before I have to beat it out of you?" looks. "You think his lucid moments are linked or synched or whatever with whenever we watch our parents in the water?"

That made Harry sit up straight and cock his head to one side, like he couldn't believe what he was hearing. Or didn't want to believe. Because I sure didn't believe.

"I'm on my way to the clinic. How much time do you have left on your shift?"

I flinched and looked down at the water. How much of Mum and Pop's activities had I missed? They were standing on the beach, looking out to the water and the sailboats on the horizon, arms around each other's waists. Just standing. They looked so peaceful. Certainly not like they were planning on doing something that would have us worried and wondering and now doing something totally bizarre, just to figure out what happened, where they went, and how to bring them home.

"About an hour, or ..." I checked my watch and Harry picked up the notebook he used to record anything we saw that might be useful later, like street signs and business names and people who had showed up before. "Forty-nine minutes, give or take."

"Okay, call me the second the vision and the water vanish. Or I'll call you, if he calms down and goes back into his trance or whatever you want to call it."

"If you're thinking what I'm thinking --"

"Then we're in really big trouble, because I've got the feeling I don't want to see inside your head, and you definitely don't want to get inside mine." Daniel ended on a chuckle.

I still felt a little insulted, even though I knew he was joking.

"Can you call in one of the people who theorized he's only half of himself, and -- I don't know -- check him somehow to see if he's more himself now, while this is going on?"

"Good idea. Let me get to work." He hung up before I could agree.

I focused on Mum and Pop in the water while I told Harry what he hadn't already guessed.

"He said once the fog took them," Harry said slowly. "What if the fog only *partly* took him?"

"And every time we're watching our folks, we aren't just watching, we're opening a window between the past and now?" I shivered and glanced up at him. "Too convenient. And scary, because think about it, we're playing with things way beyond our pay grade or anything we trained for."

"Hey, you're the one who's playing Star Trek all the time, with all its bad science," he shot back.

"You're the one who's reading all the sci-fi and looking up what's possible in all the hard science they throw at you. Seems like you should be acting as our consultant in all this."

"Yeah." He sighed, and his amusement faded like water draining from a big hole in a kiddie pool. "But what if?"

"What? Like we can reach into the vision and pull Mum and Pop out?" I shivered and looked back down into the water.

The hope and the war between belief and tossing it all away as totally ridiculous, all clear on his face, made me kind of dizzy and scared and added a few twists of guilt. It didn't matter that he was nearly thirty, he was still my little brother. I was responsible for him, just like I had been since Col. Hayward dropped that clever seven-year-old on the doorstep of our cottage in Cancun and asked us to look out for him until whatever mess his parents had gotten into resolved itself.

"I keep seeing Maurice, how he got scorched just pulling that paper out through the vision. And look what happened to that paper. We can't risk burning Mum and Pop, and who do we have to pull them out except Maurice? How could he handle both of them? Just trying to imagine being able to ... makes my head hurt."

"Like you said," Harry said softly, slowly. "Way above our pay grade. But we do know someone who has a lot more experience traveling between dimensions and stuff. Time is just another dimension, right?"

"According to Dr. Who, maybe." I looked up at him in time to see him stick his tongue out at me. That helped. We both grinned at each other. "Okay, you're right. We call in Stanzer, and hope that the Hounds can help us out, if he can't. If they're willing. He said he kind of ticked them off, with that whole stupid decoy and leading that crime boss on a wild goose chase, and they left him alone when he needed them to save his neck, so he got hurt. But getting him involved here might help him get over the whole issue with Dandova."

"Dawn. Her name here on Earth is Dawn Dover. When she comes to live here, we need to use the name she's used to."

"If she comes to live here. Just because Angela and Hayward are pulling all sorts of strings, that doesn't mean she'll agree. She could still be pretty pissed at him."

"Yeah, but it's better to be with people who understand you, who know what you're going through, even if you're screaming mad at them, than to be stuck with a bunch of people who think you're crazy if you tell them what you know."

"Hey, philosopher." I shook my head. "When did you get so smart?"

He wrinkled up his nose at me and rolled his eyes, and we just grinned at each other for a few seconds. Until I remembered I was supposed to be watching the vision in the water.

The vision died and the water vanished at three hours and two minutes. When I noted the time, Harry told me that last night's final viewing time was three hours and one minute, and the one before that was just about three hours. When had the duration slowly increased? We weren't totally accurate, down to the seconds, with recording the time. I reached for my phone, and it buzzed in my hand, then rang. Daniel.

"Sorry, we were making notes," I said, when I opened up the line, instead of saying hello.

"Okay, so that's one theory sort of proven. And your theory is right, too. He was a lot more solid, physically at least, during the duration of the vision. When the connection cut off -- how long ago?"

I checked the time with Harry. We were using the clock on Harry's phone, which was synched with the wireless signal, so it was synched with Daniel's -- same network, even the same model of phone.

"When the vision shut down and the connection cut off, it knocked him flat," he went on. "He's totally unconscious, near-comatose, just like the other times when his periods of raving lucidity ended. So the question now is, what do we do with this? How can we use it?"

"So if part of him got sucked into the fog that took my parents, in theory, how do we reunite the missing part of him and pull our parents out of it?"

"We need to get as many minds together working on this as we can. There's more room at my grandparents' place, and we're going to want to hold the meeting indoors, just to keep people from overhearing."

"We're going to want to have computers so London and Sherwood can join in, and the Colonel, because he's out of town."

"Backtracking Tucker?"

"That, and he got a lead on the Pi Surprise people. I sure hope they're not working together."

"You and me both." Daniel sighed. "Can you start making calls? I'll set things up with my grandparents, consult with the healers."

"You got it. Of course, I need to get to work pretty soon. The boss might get a little touchy if I keep arriving late every morning."

Daniel laughed, which helped for a little while. Not for long. There was so much to think about, so many freaky theories that spun off of that morning's discoveries.

~~~~~

Ever had one of those totally weird moments, when you're sure the universe is listening in, and not just listening in, but taking notes and then rearranging the playing pieces so you get smacked upside the head the next time you turn around? Or maybe there was someone on the other side of that hole we were creating in time and space, about four times a day, and they were listening and laughing at us.

We canceled the viewing session right after mine and Harry's, to give people time to work on what we had learned and theorized. Pete had the next watching shift, that afternoon. We had already determined that strong emotions helped with some of the "controls" for what we saw, the angle, and how close the vision followed someone, and if it would follow someone who moved out of our folks' general area. Because the jerk nearly killed him, Pete had a
~~~~~

strong emotional reaction every time Tucker showed up in the water vision. Several times, he had focused on Scowling Man so hard, the image followed Tucker when his path and our parents' path diverged, so Pete had to focus and bring them back into the screen, so to speak.

That afternoon, Pete was on duty with Annamarie, and she was just curious enough about Tucker, she didn't nudge Pete when the "lens" stayed on him instead of following our parents as they strolled up the beach. Tucker stomped away, then flinched and yanked his phone out of his pocket, and the perpetual scowl vanished in a look of utter fear. He ran down the beach and passed our folks. Pete was curious enough he didn't shift back to following our parents, and Annamarie let him. After all, Tucker was her patient, and anything she could learn might help him.

Tucker ran to a patio area extending from a very ritzy café. A thin, blond woman dressed all in black was waiting. Honestly, all black in that weather? It might have been okay if it was a bikini, or maybe some shorts and a glitzy T-shirt, but she was dressed in a long-sleeve shirt dress that hung nearly to her ankles when she was sitting down.

She was Kerri. From Pi Surprise. Pete was positive of it. I believed him, even if he hadn't drawn a sketch, showing Tucker standing hunched over in front of her, with sweat streaming down his face. Kerri looked cool and in control, and had this disdainful expression that made me think her blood was anti-freeze, forget about ice water.

So that answered a few questions and resulted in some really unpleasant news and branching theories. We had a better idea of who Tucker worked for: the creeps who tried to use Pete and me to give them a foothold in Neighborlee. More proof they were the organization that had attacked Neighborlee through that really weird social experiment, my freshman year of college?

At the same time, maybe this was encouraging news? If the people Kerri worked for had taken our folks, why hadn't they taken their sweaty minion, Tucker? So maybe Kerri's bosses *hadn't* taken our folks? Or maybe, even more encouraging, our folks had figured out some way to resist Kerri and Tucker's nefarious plans, and the resulting backwash from the struggle had half-phased out Tucker?

Yeah, like Harry said, way above our pay grade.

Then we had a breakthrough, though we weren't really sure what good it did us.

Kerri was interested in the beads on my keychain. The one Pete had made for me from beads Emma found. What if Tucker had been ransacking the crates of the Crowders' belongings looking for that bag of beads, when we caught him coming out of their flat? What if Tucker had seen the beads on the bracelet Jake made for Pete, and picked him up to get them? Then when we were too close, he threw Pete in the river as a distraction to make good his escape.

Mum was wearing her bracelet made of those beads in every vision in the water where Tucker caught up with my folks. What if he was looking for a chance to take the bracelet? What if the hotel room had been ransacked by Kerri's people, trying to find the bracelet after my folks vanished?

So if they were after the beads, what did they do to my folks? Did they get the beads? Was Mum wearing the bracelet when they vanished?

Was this theory anywhere near to the truth? What good did all this theorizing do us, except generate more questions?

Chapter Thirteen

I'm not going to go into all the theories and counter-theories and data people offered and objections and possible disaster scenarios we all thought up at the meeting that evening. The Sheridans were wonderful hosts, and went out of their way to make up for all the years of suspicion and utter lack of communication, when we could have been working together. They fed us incredibly well, to the point even I, with my superhero metabolism, ate more than was good for me. I couldn't remember the number of times that had ever happened to me. Maybe never.

We spent a good hour going over the data London and Sherwood generated from monitoring the energy shield surrounding Neighborlee. How that translated into our ability to resist or repel enemy invasion from the physical, earthly realm as well as from other dimensions. We now had proof that the reservoir of energy that supported our work as guardians was slowly growing. Yet despite our earlier theories, everybody who had gained the ability to see the winkies could still see them, even though the winkies had more than enough magical energy reserves to keep themselves invisible. Maurice had a few choice comments about how he couldn't escape winkies, but I noticed he didn't try to avoid them when they swirled around him. They were part of his exile, acting like monitors. He was turning out to be like the town curmudgeon who complained about cats in his yard, then was caught buying them toys stuffed with catnip.

The most important parts of the meeting happened once we caught up on what everybody had been figuring out on their own. We agreed that the next time we watched my folks, a team of healers would bring Tucker. They would monitor him to see how proximity to the water and to the viewing window into time was affecting him. They would get him out of there if it looked like being so close was harming him. We broke up the meeting around 10:30 and went home to get some sleep. It was a good thing we agreed to meet just before dawn the next morning, because I wasn't able to get much sleep at all. Better to get up and get moving than lie around in bed, tossing and turning until I nearly threw myself on the floor.

A Hound was waiting at the quarries when my brothers and I arrived. It just stood there, its huge paws on either side of the basin where we did our mixing and watching. It didn't move when Harry walked right through it and spread a couple plastic dropcloths, then some lawn furniture cushions, then blankets over them. We had learned in a long string of chilly mornings to protect ourselves from the damp. I had to bite my tongue and finally look away, because it freaked me out a little, seeing Harry and the Hound sort of overlap. Harry didn't see the Hound, of course, and I wasn't about to freak him out. When Stanzer drove up, the Hound vanished. I wasn't sure if it went away or it just stepped out of phase so I couldn't see it. I wasn't going to ask.

I asked Stanzer how things were going in the effort to bring Dawn up to Neighborlee from her orphanage south of Columbus. I had never asked how she ended up that far south, when she had actually been found in the Cuyahoga National Park near Akron. Maybe this wasn't the right time to ask. Then again, focusing on Stanzer's concerns and supporting him would be good for all of us. He seemed a little more upbeat today, and actually smiled when I asked him.

"There was an email waiting when I left the meeting last night," he said. "With Col. Hayward's character references, and our friends pulling strings ... It's happening a lot faster than it normally would. I think we've been lucky to get some reasonable people assigned to the case, and they're focused on a smooth transition for Dandova, getting her settled in before school starts. If she agrees to come up with me. She may just dig her heels in and break all ties or ..." He shrugged.

"I think it's helping enormously that everyone knows you're leaving it all in her hands," Angela said, coming up behind me. "There were a few people who thought it was rather ... how shall I say it? They feel it's thoughtless, maybe even arrogant, that John wants everything arranged before revealing the plan to Dawn. We must remember to call her Dawn, especially when we're dealing with those officials and bureaucrats. Don't generate uncomfortable questions by calling her Dandova."

"Right." Stanzer nodded.

"As I was saying, some thought Dawn should be involved in the process from the beginning. Including all the waiting and nail biting and temporary refusals and roadblocks. Most, though, are of the opinion that John is being considerate, saving her the tension of waiting. If ultimately permission is denied, and he is perhaps ordered to stay away from her until she is a legal adult, then Dawn need never know what was done and decided. She doesn't have to suffer. And John gets to do the suffering for both of them."

"I screwed up," Stanzer said. "Serves me right. We could have had a lot of help, maybe gotten things arranged right then and there when we met up the first time, but I messed it up."

"That's your opinion, and you are far too close to the situation to view it clearly." Angela patted his shoulder. "Have patience."

Then the others started arriving in clumps and there were too many of us to risk conversations. With the morning fog over the quarries and the chill in the air and the carrying properties of rock and water, we had to be quieter than normal. It was one thing for two or three people to have a conversation in the quarries, and manage to avoid the acoustic pockets that broadcast our words all over. With more than a dozen people gathered around that one little basin in the rock, everything changed. It was also easier to have two or three people split up and vanish, if rangers showed up and wondered what we were doing. Not so easy with as many people as we had there that morning.

Ford and Jinx brought the water from Jinx's pond, and Kurt and Jane brought water from Black Water. They brought three large jugs, from three different layers in the water. They thought today it might help to experiment with different waters.

I disagreed, but then, I was feeling a little nervous. Especially when Daniel's mother and the healers working under her arrived, leading a wobbly, pale, somehow shrunken Carson Tucker. Looking at him, as they gently settled him in a folding lawn chair about ten yards away from the basin, facing away from it, I found it very easy to believe part of the man was missing. He wasn't really shriveled up or shorter, he just seemed less. Even taking into account the years since the first time I saw him.

Pete looked over and watched for a few seconds, but he didn't move closer, he didn't say anything, and he didn't react. Maybe he was fighting not to show anything, not feel anything. He wasn't going to give this creep the satisfaction of bothering him. I didn't point out that Tucker seemed pretty out of it. Either his brain was in a holding pattern again, or Daniel's mother had given him a sedative to make him easier to transport. Besides, what were the chances the creep would recognize Pete after all these years, even if he was lucid when he looked at him?

Pete didn't fight me when I caught hold of his hand and held it. After a few seconds, he turned his hand around in my grip and twined our fingers.

We settled down around the basin. I was on a cushion right on the edge, with Harry standing behind me and Pete next to me, and Angela on my other side. Kurt and Jane stood behind Arthur, who hadn't asked for a front row seat, but we felt it was only right, as someone who was so supportive and had been there in Bermuda. Daniel and Stanzer stood back a step or two. I kept looking for the Hound to show up again. Athena, Wallace, Doni and Cosmo arrived last, bringing boosters for the wireless signal, fully charged computers, and some sensors Kurt and Wallace had been devising, to let London and Sherwood observe and hopefully record useful data. Nothing they had tried so far had worked to catch any of the visions in the water, but they had been learning and tweaking constantly. Today might be the day.

"Ready?" Kurt and Jinx did the honors, dipping up a cup of water at a time from each container and pouring them in together.

While they were doing that, Pete handed out copies of sketches he had made from the last image he had yesterday of Mum and Pop. Having the sketches helped everyone present focus and bring up the vision in the water almost at the same point where it had left off.

All that focusing from so many Gifted minds made a difference. The shimmering glow started up almost before the last of the water trickled into the basin. Harry grunted when the first clear feature was Tucker's scowling face. He had caught up with our folks maybe an hour after he had that fear-sweat-filled meeting with Kerri. The rest of the image gained focus and we saw our parents, walking up the beach toward an open air café that was growing familiar to all of us. That helped with focusing on the image and picking up where the last viewing session had left off. That café was obviously a favorite spot for our folks.

The sunset on the water was incredible, a dozen shades of crimson and gold and purple. I could almost feel the breezes rustling through the beach grasses and the palm trees and flapping the decorative flags hanging from poles and awnings. Funny, but I really did think I could hear voices. People walking the beach. Sitting at the tables our parents passed. Other people talking in the tiny shops or bartering with the people who sold from pushcarts all around the beach. I opened my mouth to ask if anyone else heard, or I had finally snapped a few circuits.

"Meeeeee!" Tucker wailed, and leaped up from the lawn chair. It went down with a clatter as he staggered across the ground, straight toward us.

"What is that?" Arthur pointed down into the water.

Light swirled and rose up from the image. In all the times we had been watching, I had never seen light move out of the center of the water. Now it was rising above the water.

I gagged, when I realized there was color in that light, and it was coming from Tucker's image in the water. He seemed to be stretching and sort of going pixilated -- and he was looking straight at me. I could almost believe he could see me.

Tucker shoved us aside and plunged downward, reaching for the water, all the while jabbering, "Me, me, me!"

His hand bounced off the water. He tried again, and again bounced off, but this time the image in the water rippled.

Kurt and Stanzer and Daniel grabbed hold of Tucker and dragged him away. Those streaks of light came up out of the water with him, and the Tucker in the vision in the water stood there, staring at his hand, which seemed to go semi-transparent. Streaks of light came out of his hand. Or maybe pieces of his flesh turned into light? They swirled away, up, out through the surface of the water. To our time and place.

It all happened so fast, maybe ten or fifteen seconds from the time Tucker shoved us aside and touched the images. Annamarie and her team did something. I didn't see because I was focusing on the man in the image -- and my parents, who were the only ones among the people on the beach and in the café who seemed to notice and react to what was going on. They turned and found Tucker, and they froze for a few seconds. I could tell from the movements of their eyes, they could see that light leaving him as his hand melted and flowed away.

Then Tucker went silent behind us. The Sheridan team had sedatives ready, and a healer who could touch him and put him to sleep in just a few seconds. It took a lot out of her, but her presence was vital to our effort that morning.

In the vision, Tucker staggered backward, clutching his hand to his chest. He didn't seem to be bleeding, and he grew smaller in the vision, so I couldn't see if there was any damage.

"Did anybody else see that? Did anybody else hear sounds, the people talking?" I asked, as the rest of our group reassembled around the basin. "Any chance we could -- Mum, Pop, can you hear us?"

"Lanie?" Mum turned and looked almost directly into the "lens" of the vision. Her voice sounded like it came through water. "Charlie, did you hear her?"

"Sure did," Pop said, nodding. He looked around. "Lanie, was that you? Where are you?"

"That cannot be good," Kurt murmured.

"Get back," Stanzer snapped. He pointed at me.

No, he pointed at my hands. I looked down. In all the commotion, I had been knocked off balance when Tucker pushed past us. I had put my hands on the edge of the basin. My fingers were dipping down *into* the water. They hadn't bounced off, like Tucker's hand had. The color was streaking out of my fingers, swirling down into the image.

"I can't feel my hands." I felt a giggle rising up in my chest. Either that, or I was going to heave, right into the water.

My elbows sort of unhinged and I felt myself tipping forward. I was going to face-plant right into the water.

"Lanie, where are you?" Mum said.

For a second there, so help me, I flashed to the scene in *The Wizard of Oz*, when Dorothy is locked in the witch's castle and she sees and hears Auntie Em, in black-and-white, calling for her in the big crystal ball.

Something huge and black and electric blue and full of tingling, hot energy slammed into me and knocked me backwards, flat onto my back. I banged my head on the rock of the plateau and looked up into the sparkling blue eyes of a Hound. Harry snapped off a couple Spanish curses and Pete shouted my name and everyone else was reacting, startled and confused. The Hound grinned at me, and I was afraid for about two seconds it was going to lick my face with that huge, glowing tongue. Then it just vanished. There one second, gone the next.

"What was that?" Daniel demanded. He got to me before everyone else. Even Angela seemed sort of stunned motionless for a few seconds.

"That was a Hound of Hamin," Stanzer said, joining him. The two of them lifted me up like I weighed almost nothing, and got me back into my wheelchair. For a few moments there, I felt like I had been drained until there was nothing left of me but a thin casing, like a deflated balloon.

"Wait." I finally caught my breath and got my tongue back. "Mum -- she heard me." I gestured back at the basin, and I was close enough to see the image was gone. The basin was empty.

"It just flashed and was gone when the Hound appeared," Jane told me later, when we went over the sequence of events and what everyone remembered.

I got the feeling back in my hands about the same time I caught my breath. That was a relief. I wished I had brought a sweater because I was chilled from the inside out. Angela must have seen something in me she didn't like. She declared the morning's experiment was over, and urged everyone to come back to Divine's if they wanted to have a conference. I could guess she wanted to dose me with one of her miracle teas. Yeah, I wanted that too.

When we got to the shop, Angela made a big mug of spicy tea that seemed to be mostly pepper. Maybe to mask the taste of some magical but foul-tasting herbs. I felt much better after a few slow mouthfuls, but I was content to sit and listen and let the others talk and theorize.

By that time, Tucker had been taken back to the Sheridans' clinic and Daniel's mother called to report that he had awakened much sooner than anticipated. The sedative used on him had been calibrated for the sense of solidity the healers had been monitoring. Simply put, there was *more* to Tucker now, after encountering his past self in the vision. As far as we could tell, maybe there had been some transfer of actual matter, of physical being, or at least some physical manifestation of healing. He was *more* now, and came out of his stupor enough to be coherent and ask questions. His semi-lucidity lasted twice as long as other times when he had seemed aware of the world around him.

"I hope you aren't planning on using this guy to jam the door open, and try to jump back in time and warn the Zephyrs," Stanzer said, once we had discussed that bit of news for maybe twenty minutes. Most of the discussion was whether this was proof that the vision in the water could be used as a portal, since it certainly seemed that a physical transfer had taken place. "I don't know if you caught anything from the Hound appearing, but he was scared and stern."

"All I saw was a really big bad wolf knocking Lanie flat." Kurt shook his head. "Are you saying it came on its own?"

"It was there all along," I said. "It just sort of stepped sideways, dimensionally, and was watching. You didn't ask it to knock me away from the water?"

"It did that all on its own," Stanzer said. "The message I got, more of an impression than actual words, is what a few of us have said already over the last few weeks. Time travels in only one direction. Forward. Trying to go backward will only cause all sorts of metaphysical and physics problems we don't want to even think about, much less face them."

"Forward." Arthur looked around, meeting the eyes of most of the people in Angela's living room. "They can go forward." He waited, smiling. That expression was so much like Angela's "I know something and you'd better hurry up and figure it out so I don't have to tell you" smirk, I got a little irritated with him.

"They?" Daniel said. Then he looked at me. "You think … we can bring Lanie's parents forward? And what? Protect them from whatever made them vanish in the first place?"

"What if we're what made them vanish?" Jane said.

That made everyone stop and think for a few very profound minutes of silence.

"What if we don't go in and pull them forward and pull them home?" I had to ask. "I mean, yeah, like in a lot of time travel stories, the fact that someone vanished with no explanation is kind of proof that at least the attempt was made, but like they told Lessa in the Pern books, she didn't have any proof that she succeeded. Only that she tried. What if we don't go in and even try? Will that change time, change history?"

The others discussed the options, the possibilities, the theories. Was it really time travel if my folks were basically still moving forward in time, just faster, or taking a big leap or skip or whatever the jump of twenty-some months could be called? I had to wonder if this was just reverb or some kind of reaction to the problem we had with that time traveling watch that Rita and Rodney had messed with, back in our freshman year of college. Kurt brought that up almost as soon as I thought it.

He told them about Rita and Rodney and their roommates, and then he and Ford and Angela discussed the whole stupid psycho-social experiment, and the chances that Pi Surprise was tied into the same group of enemies, maybe not affiliated with the Rivals at all. That would mean whatever we had done to win that particular battle, that team of enemies had finally recovered and were back for round two. Or maybe, since Kerri was there on the island with Tucker reporting to her, Bermuda had been round two, and the short visit of Pi Surprise earlier in the summer was round three?

The discussion didn't move back to the philosophical side of the question, and I was kind of glad. Neither of my brothers participated in that, and neither did I, after my first few questions. The thought of bringing our parents home, safely, was kind of overwhelming. Enough that it was hard to ignore the opposite possibility: the attempt to reach through the vision in the water and skip through time might just result in us losing them forever.

"You never heard any sounds before, did you?" Arthur asked, and effectively shifted the conversation away from enemies and enemy plans and tricks, back to more positive topics. Such as how all of this might be possible. There was a big difference between "if" and "how," mostly because "how" implied that the "if" was shifting into a "yes."

And more than a "yes," we were going to try.

"Nope," Harry said, when everyone turned to look at him and me and Pete. We had been spending the most time watching the vision, of course.

"What changed between today and all the other times?"

"Bigger numbers, and Tucker showing up," he said after a few moments of thinking.

Our theory: Tucker's body was trying to reunite. His present body was trying to regain what had been snatched from it, and the water vision was somehow a doorway that allowed the transfer to take place, or maybe even forced the transfer to take place. Because his partial body was there at the quarry, trying to reunite, which had caused the splintering or phasing out in the first place.

Yeah, kind of twisted, but kind of made sense, too. I almost felt sorry for Tucker.

Could we use Tucker as kind of a doorjamb, holding the portal or phased doorway open until we could reach through, or just make audible contact with my folks, and get them to come through the doorway? Come forward, without us reaching back? Because we saw how well that worked. My fingers still tingled just thinking about that fun little new experience. It wasn't like they could grab onto Tucker and let him pull them home, because obviously he hadn't vanished entirely, or we never would have found his comatose body in that Bermuda hospital.

All this theorizing was making my head hurt. Harry and Pete and Daniel and Stanzer were our nearest thing to experts, only by virtue of being avid hard SF readers. Nothing they discussed was reality, but at least they had the vocabulary to discuss it, and give it shape. The examples of admittedly fictional scenarios made it possible to try to theorize out any bugs that might get in the way.

All this time, Maurice had been sitting on top of the cabinet that served as his apartment, furnished with doll house furniture. He fluttered down now and landed on the center of the table next to a couple of plates stacked on top of each other, now that we had pretty much decimated a lot of Angela's snacks. Theorizing and plotting to challenge the laws of physics and magic tended to build up a huge appetite. He stepped up onto the stack of plates, kicked aside a few big chocolate muffin crumbs, and fluttered his wings to get attention. I got a whiff of the cotton candy scent that sometimes came off his wings. I had to agree with him, that was a particularly nasty, humiliating touch from whoever had added wings to the terms of his exile.

"Yes, Maurice?" Angela raised her hand to quiet Ford, who was worried that the park rangers were getting a little too nosey. Our days of grace in the quarries were coming to an end. All the more reason to make the big effort to rescue my folks.

"Do I need to remind you that I wasn't here on Earth when Lanie's folks were in Bermuda?" He flashed a cheesy grin at several stunned expressions around the table. "Yep, that's what I thought." He pointed at Pete, whose mouth was falling open and whose eyes threatened to be bigger than his mouth. "All that exposure to magical stuff going on, day after day, kind of builds up in the blood. Don't know how long it'll last, but for now ... Nice to meet you guys."

"How many of you can see Maurice?" Angela asked.

"I can't see this person, but I can hear him," Arthur said. Daniel seconded that.

London was participating in the conversation through Athena's tablet, but Sherwood was helping Wallace, Cosmo, and Doni to pursue some investigative theory Wallace had regarding Pi Surprise. London could neither hear nor see Maurice, but she was getting what amounted to "pings" in the magical energy sensing equipment that was still in the developmental phase. Athena could see him now. Ford and Jinx all had impressions of movement and light and even muffled sound, to let them point to the spot where Maurice stood on the table. Unfortunately, the most they got was the "wah-wah-wuh" effect that reminded me of how adults talked in the Charlie Brown TV specials.

Soon, we got back to the subject that had brought Maurice down to join the conversation. He had already proved he could reach through the vision in the water to retrieve that piece of the cursed contract. Since he wasn't on Earth at the time my parents went to Bermuda, and since the Fae realms were a different phase of time, maybe he could reach through the water in the vision and manifest physically and help guide my parents? Without getting scorched like he had the last time.

Angela very clearly regretted putting a damper on the proposal. First, there was no guarantee Mum and Pop would be able to see or hear Maurice. At the most they might be able to feel him, but he would have to jump up and down on their arms or shoulders or their heads pretty hard to get their attention. Also, there were the terms of Maurice's exile to consider. If he was blocked from going through the paintings in the attic that were portals to other worlds, chances were good an unplanned or rogue portal through time might be blocked to him as well.

I thanked Maurice for volunteering. He was very welcome to come with us and at least try.

There had been some intense whispering back and forth, which turned out to be those who could see Maurice, describing him to those who couldn't. Interestingly, it was Daniel who brought up a big question that none of us had considered yet. He thought of it when he learned how small Maurice was. For the present time, of course.

"Okay, say Maurice can go through the images in the water without no problem," he said. "But how are Lanie's parents going to travel through time and come out that little hole in the rock? What if they get stuck?"

Arthur laughed first. It was a proud laugh, and he thumped Daniel on the back, commending him for thinking of that.

So that was how we ended up using Jinx's pond for what would have to be the last viewing. We knew we were coming up close to the time my folks actually vanished. Either we would see what happened to them, who hurt them or kidnapped them, or we would be the cause of them vanishing. There was something ironic and frustrating about it. Mum and Pop would probably laugh. I hoped they would laugh. I hoped we hadn't made some hugely stupid miscalculation, and our attempt to save them would doom them to wander forever in some between layer, like a crawl space between dimensions. What could be worse than getting trapped in the darkness, maybe in the same between place as Big Ugly?

Chapter Fourteen

We got everyone involved. London calculated the dimensions and volume of Jinx's pond, so we could determine how much of the water we would have to remove, and how much water we had to bring from Black Water Pool, to have equal parts. Then we had to figure out what to do with the water we pumped out. Just let it go, soak into the soil, eventually join the water table? In some sense, that had been happening all these years already, with no negative or quirky or just plain weird results. That we knew of.

Gordon and Mandy took care of obtaining a gas-powered pump to suck the water out. They also worked with Pastor Rocky to talk to Chief Tanner and not only get his help in making sure the rangers left us alone, but started some defensive action to avoid trouble, if we destroyed Jinx's pond in the process. After all, those scientists came out every year to check the water and look for anything growing in it, and check the effects on the surrounding wildlife. They probably wouldn't be very happy to have their job taken away. Or maybe they would be? Maybe it was boring to come out every year to examine a pond and take readings that certainly didn't seem to do them any good.

Chief Tanner was a good friend to all of us, a member of our church. As soon as he heard Gordon say this was a chance to find out what happened to my parents, the Chief stopped him right there. He had to be there and wanted to help any way he could. What could Gordon say? Certainly not no, when we were asking for an awful lot. Besides, the Chief had been through enough weirdness with our group, he had some experience of his own, coming up with boring and believable explanations for the inexplicable things we were involved in.

Kurt and Jinx got hold of some of those huge sports dispensers, borrowed from the school athletic department, to fill from Black Water. Everyone else brought whatever dispenser jugs and camping water jugs or bags and stopped at Black Water to fill up before we met at Jinx's pond.

The guilty parties involved that morning included Pastor

Rocky and Chief Tanner, Gordon and Mandy, Kurt and Jane, Angela, Stanzer, Felicity and Jake, me and my brothers, Daniel and his grandparents and parents, the entire Longfellow clan, and of course Wallace and Cosmo. We also had a dozen healers from the Sheridan group to watch over Tucker, and just in case we needed them, to help my folks.

Charlotte Longfellow showed she had more common sense than all of us, after all the planning and list-making and preparing. She stopped in at my folks' farmhouse and gathered up sets of clothes and towels and shower gel for Mum and Pop. Just in case they got drenched on their way through from Bermuda. She kept aside a two-gallon collapsible camping water bottle with tap water, for washing.

We studied the ranger patrol schedule and chose to make our experiment and hopeful rescue just before dawn. Rangers were more alert in the evening for people who shouldn't be in the park and quarries. Early in the morning, when the night shift is tired and preparing to hand things over to the day shift, looked like the best time to come in down different roads, two or three people at a time, to collect quietly and prepare. The rangers most likely to be within shouting range of the quarries were Neighborlee natives. We could depend on them being influenced to stay away by several different factors. First, the defensive magic of Neighborlee. Then a really heavy dose of prayers from Pastor Rocky and the prayer team at Neighborlee Gospel Church. And if they did notice and come investigate, Angela or Chief Tanner could intimidate them to look the other way.

Besides, we chose dawn just in case the huge amount of water involved in this experiment resulted in a massive light show, either while the door was open to the past, or when everything shut down. Lights streaking through the quarries at dawn could be explained as beams from the rising sun bouncing off the water.

Gordon and Chief Tanner got to Jinx's pool an hour before the rest of us were due to start trickling in, to set up the pump and the hose to disperse the water. Kurt rigged the hose so after twenty feet, it turned into a sprinkler hose, and then after another twenty feet it branched, and branched again after ten feet, to spread out the water as far as possible. The theory was that seeping through the dirt and stone over such a long distance would filter out all the magical qualities or just plain weirdness of the water, before it joined the water table of the Metroparks.

Just setting up those hoses and arranging the muffler box around the pump engine, devised by Ford and Kurt, took up more than half an hour of that lead time. By the time my brothers and I arrived, with streaks of pink and gold licking at the edges of the horizon, the water in Jinx's pond had gone down only about two feet. I said a silent prayer of thanks that the pool was as shallow as it was, compared to other pools in the Metroparks and quarries.

Thanks to nervous excitement over what we hoped to accomplish, I didn't get much sleep last night. I was in just the right mood to think weird thoughts. What were the chances that Jinx had been influenced to mess around in this one specific spot, and all the right factors and "ingredients" were here, to create the pond, to be ready at just the right time to hopefully create a doorway to pull my parents home, out of the jaws of danger? Because yes, I really didn't like the theory that we were the ones who had created the entire mystery of my parents vanishing without explanation.

I put my philosophical thoughts aside for later. It might be something Pop would enjoy tangling with, when we got them home safe and sound. If we got them home safe and sound. *Please, God, let this work and bring my parents home safe and sound?*

Finally, the water was down far enough to turn off the pump and reduce the loudest possibility of someone official coming to investigate and interfere. While Kurt, Gordon, Ford, and Chief Tanner took care of dismantling the dispersion gear and putting the pump away, the rest of us got to work hauling the gallons from Black Water, and slowly refilling the pool. We didn't want to do it too quickly, because we still had some people who had to arrive. The most important ones, unfortunately, included Tucker and the healers handling him. We wanted everyone in place before the light show began and the doorway -- hopefully -- opened up. Maurice was primed and read to make his dive. I just hoped he wouldn't bounce off some barrier. Really, I felt sorry for him for the terms of his exile: only full size and able to be seen and heard by everyone around him four days out of the year, and the rest of the time limited to people who had some touch of magic or semi-pseudo-superhero gifts.

The plan, if Maurice managed to get through the barrier, was for him to dive into Mum's big tote bag, which I knew would have at least two pads of paper, a dozen pens and pencils, a sketchbook and micro-recorder and digital camera. We couldn't take the chance that Maurice wouldn't be able to take anything through the barrier with him, if he could get through, so he had to be able to write a note, and fast, to warn my folks what was up, if they weren't able to see him or hear him.

"Hey …" I paused, not sure if I wanted to say this aloud. No one was really listening to me, all focused on the third sports drink dispenser being emptied into the pool. "Maurice?" I was ready to use my telekinesis and tug him over closer, but he heard me and came flying over. "If you can get through the barrier, what about your clothes? They're from here, this time stream."

For the occasion, Maurice was wearing an outfit I swear I saw Ken wearing in the third *Toy Story* movie when he was modeling for Barbie. It was quite appropriate for a James Bond-type maneuver.

Maurice grinned, his mouth opened like he would make a smart-alec remark, then he froze. His face went red, as far as I could tell in all the pre-dawn weird lighting and thick shadows.

"Yeah … well … I'll just keep my backside to everybody here, and hope nobody there can see me, and you'll all get the smallest moon you've ever seen." He shrugged and tugged on his tux jacket. "Sure hope this stuff doesn't shred when it's peeled off me. Or disintegrated. I really like this. One of these days when Holly can see me, I want her to see me in this."

"I am saving you the biggest hug, next time you're full size and not squishable."

"I'll hold you to it, babe." He winked and gave me that trigger pointer finger move, and turned to fly back to his safe observation point over everyone's heads.

"Hey -- Holly? Holly Sullivan?"

He got this awful, terrified look on his face, and pressed a finger to his lips to hush me, and then flew away so fast I couldn't track his movements.

Well, that was a surprise. Maurice was interested in Holly, our faithful, clever librarian and source of all knowledge sometimes faster than Athena or London could find it on the Internet? That Holly? I had the feeling there was a great story in there, and most likely Angela was the best source. I put that question aside for later.

The pump and hoses had been stowed in Gordon's truck. Everyone was gathering around. Tucker and his entourage were arriving, coming around the barrier of bushes that the park service mistakenly believed made it harder to find Jinx's pond. The best way to make something stand out and metaphorically wave its arms for attention was to try to hide it. Especially with decorative shrubs.

"Almost there," Ford announced, from his position kneeling on the edge of the pool and looking down. I didn't know how he managed to lean that far over, almost putting his head down into where water used to be, without falling in headfirst.

We had agreed to take the water down to just over a third of its normal volume, so we would only have to replace a third of it with Black Water, and there would be maneuvering room in the hole. And if my folks somehow did come through to us, they wouldn't be over their heads in water, if the effect didn't shut down and dry up the hole in the rock immediately. We had two emergency ladders, the kind made of chains and plastic boards, ropes, and one of those plastic sleds that looked like a food service tray, to haul up anyone who couldn't climb up under their own strength. I really prayed we wouldn't need that, but it was always smart to be prepared. Pop always used to say that being prepared for any eventuality, especially a worst case scenario, usually meant that worst case didn't happen. I hoped Pop was really right in this instance.

"It's there." Kurt pointed down into the depths of the pool.

There were still about ten more gallons of water to pour in, but whatever was involved in the process of opening the viewing lens into the past, it was satisfied. The light swirled around, growing from the central ignition spark. Harry, Pete and I took our places, roughly equidistant around the pool, to give even coverage of focus. At least, that was the theory. Ford and Stanzer and Daniel, his grandparents and Angela moved in between us to sort of boost whatever signal we were generating.

This was far too important to be so iffy on so many details, but we just didn't have the time or the patience to waste in weeks of theorizing and calculating and experimenting. I wanted my folks home *now*.

Tucker moaned and I heard that familiar rattle of someone shifting in a wheelchair, trying to get more comfortable. Then the *bang-clang-bump-rattle* of a wheelchair being pushed over uneven ground. I tried to ignore his presence and focused on him as he was twenty-some months earlier, in the vision forming in the water. I concentrated on the scene as it had been so rudely shattered yesterday, to bring it back to the exact moment when Tucker had tried to dive in and be reunited with himself.

When my parents had heard me, and I had heard them call me.

There -- in the vision, at the edge of a beachfront café, Tucker staggered backwards, clutching his hand to his chest, looking kind of stunned, his eyes going blank. Mum looked into the lens or whatever it was that allowed us to see into the past. Her mouth moved, but there was no sound. I muffled a groan. No sound from the waves, from the wind in the trees and other foliage around the café, no sounds from the people.

Tucker, the physically present Tucker in the wheelchair to my right, made that wailing sound that turned into, "Meeeeee." He had good lung control. He writhed, trying to get free of his handlers. I looked at Kurt, then Felicity, who were to my left. They both nodded.

"It didn't open up until he tried to touch it," Kurt said.

"We are not lowering him down there," Ford said. "No guarantee we can get him out."

"Bring it up to him, then," Jane said.

Just to show how close to the edge of freaky-magical everything was, I saw the streamers of energy going out from Jane's head and her chest. The streamers gathered together and swooped down into the water, just above the place where the vision was expanding to fill the vastly larger area of the pond. Jane scooped up maybe two quarts worth of water in the "hands" of the Ghost field, and brought it up and out, to hover in front of Tucker.

That water swirled and sparkled and took on colors, but being so small, I couldn't make out any details. It hung in front of Tucker's face. He stilled, his eyes widened, and he got that enchanted three-year-old look on his face. He reached out and tried to hold the globe of swirling, glowing water.

"Lanie?" Mum called from the pool.

Tucker wailed and shoved the globe of water away from him.

Streaks of flesh-colored light came out of the globe and from the vision in the pool. At least, it looked like something was trying to reattach to Tucker from the past, rather than the past trying to suck him down into it. That had to be good, right?

"Mum? Pop? Can you hear me?" I nearly threw myself out of my wheelchair.

No, that wasn't me, that was something tugging on me. I gripped my chair. Daniel was on my left hand, and he stepped over and grabbed hold of my chair.

"Sweetheart, where are you?" Mum laughed a little, and looked around at the people scattered around the café. There were a few strange looks being directed her and Pop's way, but not too many. At least, not yet. People were gathering around Tucker, who was staggering away, clutching his arm to his chest. He looked terrified. The people followed him as he kept trying to retreat, stumbling over chairs, then over the edge of the pathway at the top of the beach, that separated the cafes and shops from the sand.

"You're not going to believe this, but I'm here in the Metroparks, it's August, going on two years since you and Pop left to go to Bermuda. Mum, you guys vanished before Thanksgiving, and we've been trying to figure out what happened."

Mum and Pop moved away from the crowd, heading down the beach. Most likely following the sound of my voice. But the crazy thing was that while the lens of the vision hovered in front of them, it kept moving backwards, down the beach, like it was leading my folks away from the crowds. Weird, huh?

"Vanished how?" Pop asked.

"We don't know. We just know that we're pretty close to the time that Hayward's people said you vanished. If someone attacked you, we're hoping to stop it. That guy who just went crazy? That's the guy who threw Pete off the balcony in England. He's been following you for days. He wants the bracelet Emma made for Mum."

"How do you know that?"

"Charlie, we can discuss the metaphysics and magical theories later," Angela said. "The important thing is to get you pulled forward in time before disaster strikes. If it's going to strike."

"Angela?" Mum shook her head, like maybe she was trying to clear her ears.

The image in the water kept moving as they kept walking, farther down the beach, farther away from people, heading away from the lights, into darkness.

No, there was light, coming over the ocean water. From far away. In the water?

"Just trust me, Mum, please?" I felt that pull again, trying to lever me out of my wheelchair, down into the water. "Daniel --"

"I got you." He grabbed onto my upper arm with one hand and tightened his grip on my chair with the other.

Streaks of light swirled up from the vision in the pool water. One thin streamer like a vine or a tentacle wrapped around my ankle. I gasped, or tried to, because suddenly I couldn't breathe.

That flicker of light out on the water was a boat, moving fast. It was one of those sleek black landing craft from an action thriller movie. A woman stood in the prow, dressed in black, her pale hair tied back with a scarf that half-covered her face.

I was having a vision inside the vision of my folks, and that kind of freaked me out.

The woman turned and her eyes locked with mine, and I knew she could see me, could see through time, from nearly two years ago to this moment in the Metroparks.

Kerri, from Pi Surprise.

That moment of recognition snapped the vision apart, but not before I got a glimpse into swirling darkness and ice spun through my veins. I knew what she wanted. It didn't make sense. I didn't have time to think about it. This was the time to act.

"We have to get the portal open," I wheezed, struggling to get my breath back. "That's the danger. They're coming for my folks." I reached down, and more streamers of light spun up from the water and wrapped around my wrists.

Pop let out a stream of Chinese cussing that didn't sound anything like what Mal and Jayn and Zoe said on *Firefly*. Nowhere near.

"Lanie," Mum said, her voice strained and her eyes wide, as a foggy sort of light swirled around them and partially illuminated the beach. "We can see you."

"The fog," Harry said. "The creep said they went into the fog and he was trying not to let it get him."

"What if the fog is trying to eat them?" Pete yelped. "Maybe they need to run away."

He was right. The fog was streaming across the water, coming up the beach. How could it be coming from that sleek black landing craft with Kerri, that wannabe vampire, on board? But it was.

"Come to me. Hurry. That woman in the fog is coming for you. She's Tucker's boss?"

"Who is Tucker?" Mum said.

Pop shook his head. "Forget that. Come on, babe, we've got a flight home to catch." He twined his arm with Mum's and caught hold of her hand, interlaced their fingers, and together they ran straight into the vision.

The streamers of light turned flesh-colored, and my hands went numb again. The feeling ran up my arms fast enough to scare me. Gut instinct shouted in my head, and I shouted, at the same time Angela shouted.

"Throw her in."

"Throw me in!" I twisted my shoulder from Daniel's grasp. It hurt. I knew I was going to have bruises for days. I shoved that thought aside as I used my telekinesis to reach into the vision, and to guide me as I fell, belly-slamming into the vision and water.

Mum and Pop reached out with their free hands and the fog suddenly became tentacles darting out from that oncoming boat. Streaking and writhing across the dark sands. Racing to catch them. I hit the water, hard. Light flared all around me. I bounced up, the breath knocked out of me. Like a terrified little kid -- the first, yes, the last two, no -- I reached with my arms and my mind and dug my fingers and will into my folks. Light splashed all around us, hot and then icy, and then a shimmering, chiming mist as the three of us fell down in a heap in the bottom of Jinx's pond.

The water was entirely gone. We hit sand and silt and stones and slimy water weeds. Pop got the worst of the impact, with me and Mum falling across him.

For several long moments, the only sounds were the breeze in the trees and Tucker's gasping, gagging sobs, and then the thud as he slid out of his wheelchair and hit the ground.

~~~~~

Angela always came prepared. She had restorative tea, and made sure the three of us drank a full cup before she let anyone talk. There was lots of hugging, which was great for all of us who
~~~~~

had been searching for all these months, but a little confusing for Mum and Pop, who had only been conscious of being away from us for a few weeks. In fact, in their memories, we had talked on the phone just a little less than a week ago. They couldn't argue with what we told them, about the passage of time, because yes they had just been yanked from Bermuda into the now-empty Jinx's pond.

We moved the rescue party to Divine's Emporium, because Angela wanted to dose us with more of her tea. There was more room at the Sheridans' house, but Divine's was closer. Arthur insisted on catering a celebration breakfast. Fine with me, because I was starving. The five of us crammed into my Jeep, which also suited me just fine. The closer, the better. Harry drove, because I wasn't in any shape to do it. Despite Angela's tea, I was shaking. So were Mum and Pop. We clung together in the back seat and Pete sat in the front and took over giving a running monolog on all the things that had happened since our folks vanished from Bermuda. Well, now we knew why and how. I was equally relieved and furious, to know we had most certainly needed to rescue our folks.

About the time we pulled up in front of Divine's, Pete's narration got as far as Felicity and Jake's wedding. Mum was pretty disappointed to have missed it, because she considered Felicity a daughter and would have wanted to help with the fussing. Pete hurried through the arrival of the Sheridans and the first big conference with Hoax, and the trap that resulted in pretty much shutting down the Rivals. That was while we were unloading from my Jeep and getting me into my wheelchair and going around the back of the house, to Angela's garden. It was really the only place that could comfortably hold all of us. We would just have to trust in the defensive magic of Neighborlee to keep our conference and debriefing and celebration from being overheard.

The trip from the past had drained Mum and Pop, and the effort to grab onto them with my telekinesis had drained me. Angela made the three of us come inside where she dosed us with more tea. She had us all take turns putting our hands on the Wishing Ball, and asked one of her friends on the other side to examine us and make sure we hadn't brought something unfriendly and unsuited to life on Earth through the time portal. (See? I always knew it was a communication device, and not just for wishing, or spying on people as Maurice confessed to me later, when I asked him for more details about him and Holly.) I'm sure she filled my folks in on some things Pete hadn't thought of or didn't know, during the time I was washing up and changing into some borrowed clothes. Despite the water vanishing when the vision closed, all of us had gotten wet. It wouldn't be good to leave that magically enhanced and altered water on our skin for too long. Besides, Mum and Pop had had a long day of walking beaches and sweating in Bermuda. They had been debating whether they should go back to their hotel to wash and change before getting dinner, when the whole ruckus started.

Arthur seemed to enjoy playing generous benefactor. He knew the strings to pull and people to call, and how to make people snap to it and get things done in half the expected time. Or maybe he already had a celebration feast, ready and waiting to be delivered and set up. By the time we came outside again, that was what was waiting. A celebration and welcome home breakfast. We made sure Mum and Pop were fed first, and seated. Then the introductions started, the explanations, and filling in more pieces of the stories of everything that had happened while they were gone. Athena called Col. Hayward and let him know about the rescue and retrieval.

I didn't go to work that day. That was okay, because Daniel called Conrad and told the office that a family emergency had come up and I was unavailable. He let enough slip that Conrad guessed, and around lunchtime, because yes, the party and catching up lasted well into the afternoon, Conrad and Clarice both came over to welcome my folks home. Conrad was a newspaperman, but he was a decent human being first. He promised to wait a week before doing a story in the *Neighborlee Tattler*, to give my folks time to settle in and acclimate -- and come up with a good cover story.

We certainly couldn't tell the truth, could we?

Some truth helped, and some truth just made the ordinary, everyday circumstances of being a guardian of Neighborlee a little more complicated.

As we had theorized, Tucker got put back together, mentally and physically. He was more wiped out than my folks and me combined, and it took a few days for him to recover enough to be questioned. Daniel's mother and her team spent that intervening time letting him know just what had happened to him and the big debt he owed all of us for putting him back together.

He was grateful, but more than grateful, he was terrified. Of Kerri, from Pi Surprise. He told us everything before he asked for sanctuary. In the end, we granted him protection because he did tell us the truth, everything he knew, with no strings attached.

The day we first saw him, in England, he had been searching the Crowders' shipping crates for Emma's beads. He hadn't found them, and his foul mood when he saw us was mostly from fear. The woman I knew as Kerri had implied dire consequences if he didn't find them. He was afraid to even say her name, and Annamarie suspected there was some hypnotic programming to keep him from saying it aloud. Tucker saw the simple little leather thong bracelet Pete was wearing, and picked him up to yank the bracelet off him, just as I theorized. But he didn't get the bracelet, being in too much a hurry to escape.

Kerri and Tucker and their organization focused on us, starting when Mum wore the bead necklace and earrings in the bio picture on the back of her and Pop's newest book. Kerri had sent Tucker to track down my mother and get those beads at any cost. That evening on the beach, Kerri had been coming to get the beads herself, because Tucker had failed several attempts so far, including breaking into our family home and then my folks' hotel room in Bermuda.

The irony was that all this time, the beads had been "sleeping" until enough of the beads came out into the light of day, when Pete made the bracelet for Meggie. We theorized that the focus had come on us when I wore the earrings last spring. I had participated in a charity fundraiser event put on by a handful of churches throughout Cuyahoga County, to bring attention to homeless children and the high demand for foster parents. The story had been picked up by the *Plain Dealer*, the *Akron Beacon Journal*, and a dozen other newspapers in Northeast Ohio. Then it was picked up by Fox News and a spreading ripple of online sites focusing on foster care and the homeless. Somewhere in all that, Kerri and her minions had seen the picture, recognized the beads, and knew where to come look for them.

Chapter Fifteen

Mum handed the bracelet over to Angela, to go into safe storage. Whether that would stop Kerri and her people from locating the beads and trying again, we had no idea. We could only be watchful and ready.

After all, we still didn't know the significance of the beads, their uses or magical potential. Or the danger they contained. Only time would tell. Or maybe the Fae archeologists, if they ever responded to Angela's request for information. There was that pesky time differential between Fae and Human realms, that kept getting in the way.

Mum didn't get to help put together Felicity's wedding, but she gladly threw herself into putting together the apartment for Dawn. She was of the opinion that Stanzer had messed up big-time by not at least making contact, even if he thought that if the plan failed, it was best not to let her know he was working to get legal custody of her. She wouldn't blame Dawn at all if she refused to cooperate, when Stanzer made his offer to bring her up to Neighborlee and work together to find the rest of the Hunt. London and Sherwood were making headway in tracking down the other arrivals, now that they knew not to limit their search to just the time when Stanzer fell to Earth. There were so many factors to take into account. A distinct geno-type and a somewhat limited pool of physical characteristics did help narrow down the search, but it wasn't enough. The most important clues were: A foreign language. Children who appeared in the middle of freak storms. Children with twin lines of scars on both wrists.

The power and otherworldly energy that came with the blue lightning couldn't help us in tracking the arrival of the members of the Hunt, because detecting it wasn't possible until recently. The weather satellites weren't picking up the many subtleties of details in electromagnetic energy even ten years ago that they were now. If there were eight years of difference between when Stanzer arrived and Dawn arrived on Earth, then maybe other members of the Hunt appeared twenty or thirty or fifty years before Stanzer.

Tracking down records of those arrivals would be even harder.

If anyone could do it, London and Sherwood could. They just needed time. And the more members of the Hunt we could track down, to compare stories and find more clues and variables, the better our chances.

So we had to start with getting Dandova Kale, now known as Dawn Dover, sixteen years old, about to turn seventeen, up to Neighborlee and settled in to start her senior year of high school. That was the first step.

With so many people vouching for Stanzer and with town officials signing on to help monitor Dawn's welfare, the authorities gave their approval, one after another, like a long row of dominoes falling down. I was impressed, and amazed, because I really hadn't been aware all those years ago of what my folks had to go through when they adopted me. My impression was that Mrs. Silvestri had to give permission, a judge had to sign the papers, and presto, I was Lanie Zephyr.

I was at Divine's with Mum and Felicity, going through the clothing rooms at Divine's to find some fun clothes for Dawn as welcome home presents, when we got the phone call. It took longer than I thought it would take, when Stanzer drove down to the orphanage to finally confront Dawn with his offer. I thought for sure she would argue with him, maybe resist for a while, at the very least make him sweat. Because yeah, I agreed with Mum, he should have at least contacted her, rather than leaving her in silence for the last four weeks.

Stanzer called Angela, because she was now also Dawn's legal guardian. The phone call didn't take long. Angela came into the clothing room with her serene smile just a little brighter.

"They're on their way. We have three hours to put together a welcome dinner."

We knew better than to overwhelm Dawn, so the welcoming committee was made of just the guardians, Longfellows, Zephyrs, and Pastor Rocky. Maurice hung back when Stanzer and Dawn arrived, until he could be sure a Hound wouldn't appear. He claimed the clashing energies made his wings itch. I was pretty sure he was afraid a Hound would try to eat him. If anyone, other than Jane, could catch Maurice when he was invisible and flying faster than light, it would be a Hound. I didn't blame him. I would have been afraid of the Hounds if my first encounter with them hadn't been one of them saving my life.

Pete and Doni were our first line greeters, when Angela went to meet Dawn and Stanzer at the gate. After all, they were closest to her age. Then Athena joined them, as they walked around the side of the house to the garden, where we had a picnic dinner set up. Stanzer walked her around, introducing her to everyone. Blue sparks danced along Dawn's scars when she came face-to-face with me. She caught her breath, then looked down at her wrists, then a smile crept across her face as she met my gaze again.

"Can you …"

"See the sparks?" I nodded. "Didn't Stanzer tell you about the mutants and alien visitors you're stuck living with now?"

"Mutants?" Her smile morphed into a grin, which I was glad to see she directed at Stanzer. "He told me a lot about Neighborlee on our way up, but not that." Then she caught her breath and her eyes got wide for a few seconds. "Wait, you were talking about the guardians, but I thought … I thought you were being kind of … funny," she ended with a shrug.

"Neighborlee is the weirdness capital of the state, maybe the country, maybe the world. Visitors from other dimensions fit in just fine here. You're one of us, and we're going to help you two find other members of the Hunt. And this big goofus didn't tell you about London Holiday yet, did he?"

"London Holiday from Flopdrop?" Dawn frowned and shook her head.

"Athena will introduce you. She's part of the group that created Flopdrop. More important, she helped London Holiday be born, and now the world's first Artificial Intelligence, self-willed and with a pretty cool sense of humor, is helping us out. We'll find other members of the Hunt, no matter how well they're hidden."

"Or how long ago they showed up on Earth?" Dawn's expression relaxed more. "You know a lot more about me than I know about you."

"That's because I didn't want you freaking out and jumping out the window while we were doing seventy on the highway," Stanzer said.

"But it's okay to freak out now?" Maurice said, swooping in to land on his shoulder. He waved at Dawn. "I sure hope you can see me, kid. Yeah, I think you can," he said, when Dawn took a step back and stared. "Yep, I'm real. Small but mighty."

"When you said interdimensional visitors ..." Dawn swallowed. "I thought you were just talking about us."

"Hey," I said, reaching out to catch one of her hands. "I grew up here, and I'm still learning a lot about what this town and the people living here can do. Neighborlee protects us from the outside world, and we protect the outside world from the weird and wonderful of Neighborlee. This is the absolute best place for people like us to live. You're home now, Dawn. This is where you belong."

END

Neighborlee, Ohio

(Title, Original Title, Release Date)

Confessions of a Lost Kid (Growing Up Neighborlee) 05/20
Semi-Pseudo-Superheroes (Dorm Rats) 07/20
Virtually London (London Holiday) 09/20
Living Proof (that no good deed goes unpunished) (Living Proof) 11/20
Night of the Living Proof, 01/21
Quitting the Hero Biz (Hero Blues) 03/21
Bride of the Living Proof, 05/21
Shrunk: The Exile of Maurice (Divine's Emporium) 07/21
Return of the Living Proof, 09/21
Allergic to Mistletoe (Have Yourself a Faerie Little Christmas) 11/21
Dawn of the Living Proof, 01/22
Angela's Knight (Divine Knight) 03/22
The Living Proof Gets the Blues, 05/22

ABOUT THE AUTHOR

On the road to publication, Michelle fell into fandom in college and has 40+ stories in various SF and fantasy universes. She has a bunch of useless degrees in theater, English, film/communication, and writing. Even worse, she has over 100 books and novellas with multiple small presses, in science fiction and fantasy, YA, suspense, women's fiction, and sub-genres of romance.

Her official launch into publishing came with winning first place in the Writers of the Future contest in 1990. She was a finalist in the EPIC Awards competition multiple times, winning with *Lorien* in 2006 and *The Meruk Episodes, I-V,* in 2010, and was a finalist in the Realm Award competition, in conjunction with the Realm Makers convention.

Her training includes the Institute for Children's Literature; proofreading at an advertising agency; and working at a community newspaper. She is a tea snob and freelance edits for a living (MichelleLevigne@gmail.com for info/rates), but only enough to give her time to write. Her newest crime against the literary world is to be co-managing editor at Mt. Zion Ridge Press and launching the publishing co-op, Ye Olde Dragon Books. Be afraid … be very afraid.

www.Mlevigne.com
www.MichelleLevigne.blogspot.com
@MichelleLevigne

Also by Michelle L. Levigne

Guardians of the Time Stream: 4-book Steampunk series
The Match Girls: Humorous inspirational romance series starting with **A Match (Not) Made in Heaven**
Sarai's Journey: A 2-book biblical fiction series
Tabor Heights: 20-book inspirational small town romance series.
Quarry Hall: 11-book women's fiction/suspense series
For Sale: Wedding Dress. Never Used: inspirational romance
Crooked Creek: Fun Fables About Critters and Kids: Children's short stories.
Do Yourself a Favor: Tips and Quips on the Writing Life. A book of writing advice.

Killing His Alter-Ego: contemporary romance/suspense, taking place in fandom.
The Commonwealth Universe: SF series, 25 books and growing
The Hunt: 5-book YA fantasy series
Faxinor: Fantasy series, 4 books and growing
Wildvine: Fantasy series, 14 books when all released
Neighborlee: Humorous fantasy series
Zygradon: 5-book Arthurian fantasy series
AFV Defender: SF adventure series